Daniel Johnson

**The Political Comedy of Europe**

Daniel Johnson

**The Political Comedy of Europe**

ISBN/EAN: 9783744771283

Printed in Europe, USA, Canada, Australia, Japan

Cover: Foto ©Andreas Hilbeck / pixelio.de

More available books at **www.hansebooks.com**

# THE

# POLITICAL COMEDY

OF

# EUROPE.

BY

# DANIEL JOHNSON.

London:

SAMPSON LOW, MARSTON, SEARLE, & RIVINGTON,

CROWN BUILDINGS, 188, FLEET STREET.

1880.

LONDON:
GILBERT AND RIVINGTON, PRINTERS,
ST. JOHN'S SQUARE.

*This book is dedicated to the statesman whose policy has done the most towards the growth and ripening of the European Democracy*

## THE PRINCE CHANCELLOR OF GERMANY.

*To the German Democracy, particularly, the author sends greeting and kindly sympathy, and a wish that it may acquire wisdom and the practical spirit necessary to its triumph, which alone can insure peace to all nations, and security to Europe.*

DANIEL JOHNSON.

DENVER CITY.
*January 1st,* 1880.

# THE POLITICAL COMEDY OF EUROPE.

---

## PROLOGUE.

### CHARACTERS OF THE PROLOGUE.

THE AMERICAN PUNCHINELLO.
DANIEL JOHNSON, *Author.*
JEAN DURAND, *Frenchman residing in America.*

*A public square in Denver City, Colorado.   At the back, under the trees, a theatre of marionnettes. A crowd gathered in front of the theatre.*

THE AMERICAN PUNCHINELLO: Decidedly, things are going badly in this country.  If this state of affairs keeps on, I shall most certainly complain to the Great President, Him whose thankless task it is, to govern all humanity, black and white, lords and ladies, men and beasts; to Him, I say, shall I complain of

B

my European brother's heartless competition. Yes, Polichinelle, Hans Wurst,[1] Harlequin, Petrowska, Pasquino, all of you who are showing off, on the other side of the Atlantic; you are going too fast. For years past you have done nothing but break heads and arms and legs, of actual flesh and blood, and for this you have never yet had a deservedly good licking. Whereas, poor Punchinello in America is unmercifully lynched, for having demolished a few pasteboard or wooden arms and legs, perhaps under the influence of a legitimate glass of whiskey. God is not just; no, I must surely ask of our good President a passport for Europe, where my equals all wear gilded coronets and flowing plumes, sit upon their thrones, attended by brilliant and resplendent escorts, are treated as kings and princes, and enjoy all the consideration and respect due only to those whose might makes right, by their ability to maltreat their fellow creatures according to their deserts . . . .

(*Exit* PUNCHINELLO.)

*Laughter and applause in the audience. Two of*

---

[1] Hans Wurst; *Anglice*, John Sausage, the German *Punch.*

*the spectators,* DANIEL JOHNSON *and* JEAN DURAND, *leave the crowd and come forward.*

JOHNSON : Am I mistaken ?  Surely this is Jean Durand !

DURAND : The same, my good friend.

JOHNSON : You have just returned from Europe ; you surely can verify our Punchinello's griev-ances.  Listen !  Often in watching this puppet show I have thought of the sad drama that is passing in Europe.  This thought kept knock-ing so at my brain, that from it, one day, like Minerva from the head of Jupiter, issued a grand play, filled with history and imagination, both of which, I may say—modesty apart—spread more good, sound ideas, than the usually-accepted twaddle of pedants and diplomats. This play I offered to the Denver City Theatre, and wonderful to relate, notwithstanding the lengthy passages, the lack of didactic rules, and the hard truths, in which the work abounds—they accepted it.  But, although I have made a serious and conscientious study of passing events, still there are gaps which you can help me fill. You have just returned from Europe, where you have seen near by what I have had to judge of from afar.  You will be a sort of Providence

for me, my dear Durand, if you will occasion-
ally be my prompter.   Will you help me ?

DURAND : Yes, indeed, but I fear that you will
stir up some sad souvenirs in my memory.
Remember, I am a Frenchman !

JOHNSON : You will have the satisfaction of seeing
crushed and disgraced, the so-called great
men, who are simply in God's hands what the
executioner is in the hands of human justice.
Great events can be better judged from a distance.   Between Mount Harvard[2] and Europe,
as between two well-regulated spirits, American
and European, there is distance enough for us
to fully appreciate the sad spectacle of the late
German war.

DURAND : Tell me something of your plan.

JOHNSON : Well ; first act, Bertrand and Raton.

DURAND : Bertrand and Raton ?

JOHNSON : Yes ; have you forgotten the fable of
the Monkey and the Cat ?

DURAND : Of course ; that is Prussia and Austria
in Denmark ; go on.

JOHNSON : Second act : Bertrand eats Raton.

DURAND : True, Raton brought it on himself.

JOHNSON : Third act : Bertrand watches another

---

[2] The highest mountain in Colorado.

Raton — who should have prevented the slaughter of his brother—and eats him in the next act.

DURAND : As a preliminary to eating all the rest. Do you know, Raton is a most common nickname among the diplomats. Alas, poor France, you have paid too dear for your blindness and vanity. What a sad ending !

JOHNSON : That is not the end. There are five acts, as in every respectable tragedy. But I must leave something to your imagination, and to that of the audience, who are listening to us.

DURAND : You are perfectly right. I am at your service.

JOHNSON : Now, ladies and gentlemen, I ask your indulgent attention, and —— go ahead !

END OF THE PROLOGUE.

# ACT I.

## Dramatis Personæ.

WILLIAM I., *King of Prussia.*

COUNT OTTO VON BISMARCK, *his Prime Minister.*

COLONEL HERZOG, *of the Royal Guard of Prussia.*

TRÜBE, *Chief of Police, Bismarck's Agent.*

LOREMBERG, *Jewish Banker, Bismarck's Agent.*

DR. FÜRST, *A Pan-Germanist.*

HERR WALTER, *a Berlin Merchant.*

FRAU WALTER, *his Wife.*

WILHELMINE, *their Daughter, married to M. Didier, a Frenchman.*

PETRUS WALTER, *Lieutenant, afterwards Captain in the Royal Guard.*

BARON DE MONTALBAN, *French Diplomat.*

LOUISE, *his Daughter.*

FRAU GOSCHEN, *owner of a brewery in Berlin.*

JOHANN, *an Artilleryman* ⎫
FLORA, ⎬ *her Children.*
          ⎭

SCHWARTZ, *President of the Students' Fortschrittsverein.*

THE FOREMAN OF THE BREWERY.

HERZ, *a Workman, a Socialist.*

FLITZ, *an American by birth and naturalization, but of German parents. The nephew of Frau Goschen.*

ARISTIDES, *coloured servant to Flitz.*

HERR WALTER, FRAU WALTER, *and their children.*

*The scene is laid in Germany, about 1863, before the Schleswig-Holstein war. The sitting-room of Herr Walter, in Berlin. Herr Walter's children are around him. Christmas eve.*

ONE OF HERR WALTER'S DAUGHTERS (*age fifteen*): Good evening, dear papa, Heaven's blessings upon you!

HERR WALTER: God bless you, my darling.

(*He kisses her.*)

ANOTHER DAUGHTER: Good evening, papa.

(*The children each in turn kiss their father and mother.*)

FRAU WALTER: Now for the absent ones; here is a letter from Max. He writes from Vienna, and says that he and his family are all well, and that he hopes, by next summer, to be able to pay us a visit. In the meantime he sends love and kisses to all.

ONE OF THE SMALLER CHILDREN: Dear mamma, you can tell Max that Lili sends him a kiss through you. (*She kisses her mother.*)

THE OTHER CHILDREN: So do I! so do I!

FRAU WALTER: Carlotta writes from London her

regret at not being able to pass Christmas with us, owing to her husband's delicate health.

ONE OF THE DAUGHTERS: And no letter from Paris? Can Wilhelmine be ill?

PETRUS WALTER: What was the date of her last letter, mother?

FRAU WALTER: About a fortnight since.

PETRUS (*aside to his mother*): Did she speak of Mlle. de Montalban?

FRAU WALTER. So; you are still in love with this pretty French girl?

PETRUS: More than ever!

FRAU WALTER: And have you any reason to believe that she cares for you?

PETRUS: I hope so.

FRAU WALTER: Well; there are two new weddings in prospect in our family!

PETRUS: Two! Whose is the other?

FRAU WALTER: Ah! I have not yet told you, that your brother Joseph hopes to marry a charming girl, in Copenhagen; in fact, his employer's daughter.

HERR WALTER: God bless us all. This is my recompense for the lessons of virtue and hard work, which I have given you, and to which you have so well listened. My children, always walk in the straight path, work hard and fear God, and you will not want for His blessings.

*(A knock is heard at the door.)*

ONE OF THE CHILDREN: Come in!

## SCENE II.

*Enter* WILHELMINE *and* LOUISE DE MONTALBAN.

ONE OF THE CHILDREN: Oh! it is Wilhelmine. What a delightful surprise!

*(Runs to kiss her.)*

PETRUS: But she is not alone. *(He steps forward eagerly.)* Louise! Mademoiselle!

WILHELMINE: Yes, I wanted to surprise you, and I have brought with me one of my best friends, Louise de Montalban.

LOUISE: My father will arrive here to-morrow on his way from St. Petersburg, and I was only too glad to avail myself of Mme. Didier's company, to come and surprise him, by meeting him half way.

PETRUS: Your father will not be the only one to whom your presence is an agreeable surprise. See how happy we all are to have you with us.

WILHELMINE *(gaily)*: Come, my pretty maid, lay aside your astonished manner. You will soon find that the Prussians are not such ogres as the French imagine. Give a nice French kiss to all these little Germans, who are awaiting it. Friendly relations between families go a great way towards securing national friendships.

FRAU WALTER: Well, then, my daughter, no one will have contributed more to this universal peace than ourselves; for I fancy, that soon I shall have grandchildren in all the capitals of Europe.

WILHELMINE (*laughing*): And who knows, mother, what the future may bring forth here?

(*Looking towards Petrus.*)

HERR WALTER: No news from Joseph?

(*A letter is brought in.*)

ONE OF THE CHILDREN: Here is a letter, papa; postmarked Copenhagen.

(*Herr Walter reads the letter; an expression of anxiety covers his face.*

FRAU WALTER: Is he ill (*quickly*)?

HERR WALTER: No; read it (*gives the letter*).

FRAU WALTER: What! war with Denmark! Can it be possible?

PETRUS (*with a satisfied air*): Ah! that is what Joseph writes. It is more than possible, mother dear, it is inevitable. The Danes have oppressed our German brethren in the Duchies too unmercifully. There must be an end to this, and the whole German population will joyfully, and with light hearts, enter into this holy war!

FRAU WALTER: Ah! Petrus, we can submit to war, as a necessity, courageously; but do not speak of undertaking it with joy, for the most just and most 'glorious war is but a horrible disaster!

WILHELMINE: Mother is right, and often I have been sorry to hear Petrus express these belligerent feelings. Brother, is it not enough to defend your country, when she needs your services, without for ever entertaining such hostile sentiments to others?

LOUISE: I agree with you perfectly, dear friend. I most certainly hate all wars, and all false glory.

PETRUS: Well; here you are abusing war, and all forming a coalition against me. I give in. Peace! Peace!

WILHELMINE: We grant it, if the powers that be will only grant it to all the world.

FRAU WALTER: Think of it! This very war, as yet in perspective, threatens to destroy your own brother's future happiness. He writes that since these rumours of war everything is changed. His future father-in-law, and even his *fiancée* have begun to treat him coldly. His position, already an awkward one, will become much more so—in fact, an impossible one, if this war takes place. His letter is very sad, for I imagine he is very much in love with this young Danish girl.

PETRUS: That only goes to prove that she does not love him.

WILHELMINE: There, I think you are unjust. I saw her the last time I was at Copenhagen, and I must say I was much struck by her manners and delicacy of feeling.

LOUISE: You think then, Lieutenant, that men alone have the right to love their country ?

PETRUS: I will think nothing at all, my dear ladies, which may displease you. Once more I haul down my flag, and only regret too sincerely the cloud cast over our common joy by my poor brother's letter.

FRAU WALTER: Now, children, attention !

*The door at the back of the scene opens, disclosing a beautiful Christmas tree. The children rush in, followed by their father and mother, and Wilhelmine.*

## Scene III.

### Louise *and* Petrus.

Petrus : Ah ! mademoiselle, what pleasure to see you here in Berlin ! How grateful I am . . . .

Louise : Do you for one moment imagine, my good sir, that I came to Berlin to see you ?

Petrus : Indeed, I am not so conceited. I should be only too happy, did I believe that I was once in your thoughts during your journey here.

Louise : Well, be happy. I did think of you for one minute—perhaps two ; and I just missed not coming.

Petrus : You are a darling . . . .

*He tries to seize her hand, but she runs off laughing to join Wilhelmine.*

## Scene IV.

### Petrus *and* Colonel Herzog.

Herzog (*stopping, by a gesture,* Petrus, *who is about to follow* Louise) : One word, Lieutenant.

PETRUS : You here, Colonel !

*(Makes a military salute.)*

HERZOG (*very stiffly*) : Yes, Lieutenant. You have a brother employed in a banking-house in Copenhagen ?

PETRUS : Yes, Colonel.

HERZOG : Well ; General von Roon, our excellent Minister of War, has, at the request of Count von Bismarck, chosen you to go to Copenhagen, as Military Attaché of Legation. The Minister now awaits you, to give you his instructions.

PETRUS : Very well, I will go at once. I shall only stop one moment to say good-bye to my family.

HERZOG : When it is question of the King's service, there is no such thing as family !

*(Herzog leads him off.)*

## Scene V.

*Enter* WILHELMINE *and* LOUISE.

WILHELMINE : Where is Petrus ?

A SERVANT : He has just gone out with Colonel Herzog.

WILHELMINE : Did he say nothing ?

A Servant : Nothing, madame. The Colonel carried him off for the King's service.

Louise : What does all this mean ? The King's service must be very pressing. Ah ! my dear, I feel homesick.

Wilhelmine : Patience, my friend, Petrus himself will soon be here to solve this riddle.

(*A servant brings a letter, Wilhelmine opens it.*)

Wilhelmine (*reads*) :- " Colonel Herzog von der Kreussen, to satisfy a desire expressed by Lieutenant Petrus Walter, has the honour to inform the Walter family, that the said lieutenant will for some time be detained for the King's service ; and, further, that there need be no cause for anxiety, even though several weeks should pass without news from him.

" (*Signed*) Herzog von der Kreussen."

Louise : Oh ! what a pleasant person, this colonel ! Do you often have such sudden disappearances in Prussia ? . . . . Ah ! my dear friend, there must be something behind all this ; it makes me shiver.

## SECOND TABLEAU.

*The preparations for war against Denmark.*

### SCENE VI.

SCENE: *The King's study, in the palace at Berlin. The King and Count von Bismarck are seated at a table.*

THE KING: Well, Herr Graf, how go our affairs?

BISMARCK: Everything just as you could best wish, sire. The *Nationalverein* and the old driveller who makes Frankfort his headquarters are most admirably advancing the realization of our plans. Our docile professors have for some time been preparing the way. Did not the treaties of 1326 and 1460, which consecrated the union of the Duchies, establish the 'rights of Germany, and make them as clear as the day? Since Schleswig and Holstein cannot be parted, and as Holstein is German, how can Germany give up Schleswig? And then, was it possible to miss this opportunity to capture Kiel, and loudly proclaim our *right* to the Northern Sea, the German Ocean? To-day the whole of Germany is up in arms against Denmark.

THE KING: But Austria?

BISMARCK: Austria? I have persuaded her to side with us.

THE KING: Ah!

BISMARCK: At first she hesitated. But could she give us all the prestige, in the eyes of the German people? Now you see why I have pressed the *Nationalverein* and the Diet so hard. In short, I have here a letter, from my colleague at Vienna, which promises the assistance of the Austrian forces, as soon as the Diet shall have voted the federal execution.

THE KING: When will this happen?

BISMARCK: In a few days.

THE KING: I hear that the Danish are willing to evacuate Holstein to escape a war.

BISMARCK: They are capable of doing so; but this clumsy ruse of the Copenhagen tyrant will not stop us. The national German sentiment would push us—Austria and ourselves—irresistibly forward.

THE KING: Evidently; but what I fail to understand is, that you seem to favour the pretensions of the Duke of Augustenburg. If we take the Duchies, you may be sure it is not to give them away again to any one.

C

BISMARCK : Do you think me crazy, sire ? Can you not see that Augustenburg only appears for the purpose of still more muddling what can be truly called the *most* tangled of diplomatic tangled skeins mentioned in history— truly the modern Gordian knot, to be severed by the Prussian sword. We can always get rid of Augustenburg, notwithstanding the support of the Diet, when the two combined have helped us to get rid of the others. Besides, the judges of the Prussian Crown will at the last moment show themselves sublimely impartial. They will reject Augustenburg, Oldenburg, and even Brandeburg.

THE KING : But then the lawful possessor will be the King of Denmark.

BISMARCK : Certainly ; only the judges will not give their judgment until the tyrant has renounced all his rights ; and we, having ousted him, and holding as ours the Duchies, will have long to wait to find any one powerful enough to take them from us. Besides, they will be all the more lawfully ours, we having taken them from their lawful owner !

THE KING : And how shall we settle with our allies, the Austrians ?

BISMARCK : Their turn will come to be—*Augustenburged*.

THE KING : *Augustenburged ?* Ah, I see. You are as gay as a Frenchman. (*The King rings, and orders some wine to be brought.*) Your good health, Herr Graf!

BISMARCK : Your very good health, sire !

THE KING : What date have you fixed upon for the mobilization ?

BISMARCK : There is plenty of time. A good lot of writing has yet to be done. *Cedant arma togæ.* Before we can try our Dreyse rifles on the Danish troops the whole of Europe must thoroughly understand that the Duchies are oppressed, and that we are only resisting an unjust aggression.

THE KING : But suppose they should not declare war ?

BISMARCK : I should like to see *that*.

THE KING (*after a moment's thought*) : You think, Herr Graf, that none of the powers will interfere with us in our operations against Denmark ?

BISMARCK : None, sire.

THE KING : And the English ?

BISMARCK : Palmerston is too old, and, what is

more, feels isolated. England, abandoned by
France in the Crimea, paid her back in the
late Polish rising, and still later in Mexico.
Napoleon will be only too glad of this slap at
England, to let us take Denmark. We must
divide others, or share in their divisions. *This*
is politics in a nutshell.

THE KING: You may also number among our
faithful friends Queen Victoria and the Prince
Consort. He is a true and loyal German;
he understands, and tries to make the English
understand, that a united Germany, under
Prussian rule, is the true road to European
liberty; especially, as against France to-day,
and Russia to-morrow—leaving aside the consequences—the safest for British interests. By
the way, do you not know of some nice German
prince for her Britannic Majesty's youngest
daughter? Matrimonial alliances often result
most beneficially.

BISMARCK: I will think of it, sire.

THE KING: It is a great pity you did not prevent
the Prince of Wales's marriage to that little
Danish girl; she can only have a bad influence over him. At any rate, don't let her
sister marry the Czarewitch. Are you not

afraid that Russia will not put obstacles in our way ?

BISMARCK : Your nephew, sire, on the throne of Russia, is too devoted to you and your interests. He will never prevent our staking out the road, at the end of which every true German patriot can see the Baltic transformed into a Prussian lake.

THE KING : And the French ?

BISMARCK : You may be easy on that point, sire. Napoleon will be only too glad to play the English a trick, and, further, rather dreads a fight against Austria and Prussia combined. Has your Majesty forgotten that, sometime since 1857, Napoleon, in a conversation with the Prince Consort, at Osborne, favoured the annexation of Holstein to Prussia, and was only doubtful of England's opposition on account of the port of Kiel ? Besides, that Parisian potentate has, just now, other fish to fry. In going into Mexico he ran a thorn into his side, the pain of which he will appreciate more thoroughly when the Union troops shall have completely wiped out the Southern Confederacy. As for his Italian war—well, we can say nothing. The theory of nationalities, which was the cause or pretext, will be our grand war-horse. By this, and our own energies, added to iron, blood, and nerve, will Germany establish a union.

THE KING: Say, rather, that in making use of this, Prussia *must* attain, first in Germany, afterwards in the whole world, the position to which her powerful military organization entitles her, and on which the God of armies showers his blessings.

BISMARCK: That is exactly as I understand it, sire.

THE KING: For, Herr Graf, I am rather cautious of these theories, fit more for adventurers like Napoleon. Should we seem to think too seriously of them, what answer could we make to the Poles at Posen, were they to ask for an application of them in their own case?

BISMARCK: We should send Von Moltke with the answer.

THE KING: Does not the persistent opposition of the Landtag worry you?

BISMARCK: Not a bit. First, let us conquer the Danes, afterwards others, and you will soon see these parliamentary wranglings stop of their own accord. The liberals, like all the rest, are allowing themselves to be carried away by the smoke of military glory. Ideologists are always a dangerous element in a community; happily they are usually more fools than knaves. Ours wish for the union of Germany to realize their dreams of liberty. We wish for the union, in that it will teach reason to these ideologists, who too often abuse the indulgence of our minor princes. In putting Prussia at the head of Germany, we make Germany the first nation in the world. This done, we shall then see who is right—the dreamer of Paris who puts all his trust in national sovereignty, or the august monarch who, when he took the crown from the altar at Königsberg, declared that he would govern his people by the grace of God, and sneered at the vain clamours of European Liberalism. The foundation of Prussian politics is not laid in a quicksand; rather in a mission confided by God to the noble house of Hohenzollern. For the accomplishment of this we must stand firm. Be firm, Sire! be powerful! and every opposition will come crouching at your feet. Our enemies of to-day, like those of 1848, will become our most useful auxiliaries. Might

makes right; and in might are the only ways
and means for serious politics.

THE KING (*pouring out more wine*): Your good
health, Herr Graf!

BISMARCK (*rising*): Salve, Imperator Germaniæ!


## SCENE VII.

*The same,* TRÜBE, FRAU GOSCHEN, *then her son,*
JOHANN.

TRÜBE: A woman insists upon presenting, herself,
a petition to your Majesty.

THE KING: Let her come in. (*Enter* FRAU GOSCHEN.).
Why! I know this woman. It is the good
hostess of the Brewery of the Grenadier Guards.
How can I serve you, Frau Goschen?

FRAU GOSCHEN: Sire, I have a son whom I love
better than all the world.

THE KING: I know him; it is Johann, a brave
artilleryman.

FRAU GOSCHEN: Well, sire; I know that he is
going to the war in Denmark. For Heaven's
sake, let him stay here.

THE KING (*severely*): Is he here?

TRÜBE: Sire, he followed his mother to prevent
her making this appeal.

THE KING: Bring him in. (*Enter* JOHANN.)
Johann, your mother begs me to let you stay
at home while Germany is at war with another
country. Is this also your wish?

JOHANN: Forgive her maternal anxiety, sire; I
only ask to fight in the foremost rank, for my
king and for my country.

THE KING: Well said, Johann! You shall go
among the first, and with the rank of sergeant.

JOHANN: Many, many thanks, your majesty.

CURTAIN.

## Interlude.

DURAND: I congratulate you, my dear friend.
But, tell me, what is going on now?

JOHNSON: Well, when Bismarck has proven to
the whole of Europe that the king of Denmark
(the most inoffensive of the European monarchs)
is a fearful tyrant, Prussia and Austria, having
usurped the place of federal troops of the
Duchies, by force of numbers and military
superiority annihilate the Danish army. As

the chassepots at Mentana, the Dreyse guns at Düppel prove most effective. Notwithstanding the courageous fight made by this handful of people, the other European powers, like great overgrown children, look on coldly at this, Hans Wurst's first iniquity.

DURAND: We know all that. The Schleswig-Holstein war is ancient history; what else?

JOHNSON: The war is over; here is a hero just returned.

### THIRD TABLEAU.

*After the war.*

### SCENE VIII.

*The garden of the Grenadier Guards' Brewery, owned by* FRAU GOSCHEN.

### FRAU GOSCHEN *and* JOHANN.

JOHANN (*in the uniform of an artillery sergeant; one eye out, and one sleeve empty*): Hurrah for Germany! Here I am, back again, mother. We have conquered!

FRAU GOSCHEN (*weeping*): Yes, but in what a sad plight you are, my poor boy!

JOHANN: Do not weep, dear mother; I have paid my debt to my country. If I have an eye and an arm the less, Prussia has two more provinces.

FRAU GOSCHEN: What difference does that make to me, if you are bound to drag out a miserable existence? Will Prussia be any better off with two additional provinces?

JOHANN: Well, do not talk about it, mother; you evidently do not understand the necessity of policy. How is Gretchen?

FRAU GOSCHEN: Gretchen! Did you not receive my letter?

JOHANN: Is she ill?

FRAU GOSCHEN: Ah! my poor boy, when we received the news that you were wounded her grief overcame her; she took to her bed, and . . .

JOHANN: She is dead!

FRAU GOSCHEN: She does not grieve now.

JOHANN: Good God! (*He is very much agitated for a moment.*) My sister Flora, is she still lamenting her betrothed, Scholler?

FRAU GOSCHEN: At first she was in despair at his death; then her grief changed to a calm indifference to everything about her; one

would think her faith in divine justice dead.
Her heart seems to have grown fifty years
older. Her quiet now frightens me.

JOHANN: Some other man will make up for the
loss of the first.

FRAU GOSCHEN: Who knows?

JOHANN: Is that she talking to a young man over
there?

FRAU GOSCHEN: Yes; and with her is her cousin,
Flitz, my brother's son. He is soon to return
to his adopted country, America, for which he
has been fulfilling a mission here. The coloured
man you see is his servant. Flitz, I imagine,
is trying to console Flora; I wish him success.


SCENE IX.

*The same.* FLORA, FLITZ, *and* ARISTIDES.

FLORA (*looking coldly at Johann*): Ah! there you
are, brother! Well, shout Hurrah for Germany! Scholler, it seems, was luckier than
you, for he was killed all at once.

FRAU GOSCHEN (*aside to Johann*): That is the
way she speaks now. Forgive her grief,
Johann.

JOHANN : Poor sister. (*Embraces her.*) (*To Flitz*)
Here you are, back again, cousin; and just in
time to salute the first victory of the German
Renaissance.

FLITZ : Ah, my friend, do not speak of it; I am,
like our illustrious Heinrich Heine, a *freed*
Prussian; and although conscious of a strong
affection for my first country, the country of
my fathers, I cannot applaud the aggressive
and warlike policy of the government, nor
regret having become one of the American
family.

JOHANN : But they also fight over there.

FLITZ : Very true; they are even at it now; and
I acknowledge that our civil discords furnish
a sad drama for the whole world. But it is a
passing accident, and we are not for ever at
war, like the Europeans, who are born in
uniform, booted and spurred, as if their destiny
were simply to destroy each other. The war
in America once ended—and it soon will be—
we will only struggle, as of old, to benefit our
agriculture, and develope our industries and
commerce; and on this ground, if you do not
look out, America will beat the old World, as
badly as you have just beaten the Danish.

With all this, we do not neglect spiritual and social advancement. We worship the God of justice and of work; whereas, you, owing to the pompous twaddle of your august sovereign, only know of the God of strength—the God of armies. Pah!

JOHANN: Then why do you come back to this country, for which you have such contempt?

FLITZ: If my pretty cousin Flora will listen, with your permission I will tell *her*.

FRAU GOSCHEN: Certainly.

JOHANN: *Au revoir*, cousin.

FLITZ (*to Aristides*): Leave us. (*Exit Aristides.*)


## SCENE X.

### FLITZ *and* FLORA.

FLORA: What do you want of me, cousin?

FLITZ: You have surely seen, dear Flora, during the past fortnight, what my feelings are for you, as you must easily guess the question I would ask.

FLORA: Yes.

FLITZ: And your answer is—— ?

FLORA: No.

FLITZ: Why?

FLORA: For your good as much as for mine. We would only make each other unhappy. I am soured with grief. Forget me, that is the best thing you can do.

FLITZ: I read this in your heart, dear Flora, even before you spoke. I know through what suffering and anguish you have passed. I can see the gulf yawning before you, and I can save you if you will only let me, for my own happiness.

FLORA: But I will not let you. No, Flitz, you would hazard too much. I am moved, but not decided, by your kind thought of me. War, which kills and mangles men, has also many hard blows for womankind. It has only deprived my brother of an eye and an arm, but from me it has taken my heart. I have none now. Feel! (*she presses his hand against her heart*).

FLITZ: Come with me to America, Flora. I will answer for your speedy cure. When you have once had a taste of our healthy laborious life on our model farms of the far West, you will revive. You say your heart is dead; you will soon feel a new one beat. Like our American

women, you will delight in finding yourself
grow younger, with the children God will send
you; you will live again in them, loving,
cherishing, and caring for them.

FLORA : All this is very charming, Flitz, but
does not tempt me. I am as incurable as this
old Europe, which you so justly scorn. Scorn
me also, for I deserve it; you see I have one
good feeling left, as I cannot trifle with such
honest affections as you offer. An irresistible
instinct prompts me to be revenged upon
society, for the pain I have suffered. It is all
very pretty to moralize; the world is for the
powerful and clever. Farewell, cousin, my
evil genius has got the better of me. For
your own sake pray that you may never see
nor hear of me again. (*Exit.*)

FLITZ : Poor child !

## SCENE XI.

### TRÜBE *and* LOREMBERG.

TRÜBE : Do you know that young girl who has
just left our American friend ? I fancy I have
seen her before.

LOREMBERG: Certainly, your Excellency, it is Frau Goschen's daughter.

TRÜBE: She has fine eyes, Loremberg.

LOREMBERG: I don't think she would be angry with you for saying so. Her betrothed was killed at Düppel. It seems as if, in women's hearts more than elsewhere, extremes meet; for, after having cried her eyes almost out about this fellow, now she seems only too eager to be *consoled.*

TRÜBE: Don't lose sight of her, Loremberg; we will speak of this again. (*Exeunt.*)


## SCENE XII.

ARISTIDES *has been listening to what has passed, and now enters.*

ARISTIDES: Massa Flitz had narrow 'scape dat time. Dese white folks is mighty queer. If massa lays down his stick some woman will take it up and beat him. Golly! de Lord made de white man to boss de nigger, but it makes dis nigger laugh to see de way Miss Flora can boss Massa Flitz.

(*Exit, chuckling to himself.*)

D

## FOURTH TABLEAU.

*The Students' Commers.*[a]

### SCENE XIII.

*The great hall of the " Germania Victrix " Brewery.
The waiters are arranging the tables and
benches.*

FLITZ *and* ARISTIDES; *then* SCHWARTZ *and the*
STUDENTS, TRÜBE, LOREMBERG, HERZ, *and
others.*

ARISTIDES : Beg pardon, Massa Flitz ; heard
some one talkin' about a picnic here to-night.
Foxes, wolves, music, and perhaps a fight.
Better stop and see the picnic, massa.

FLITZ (*to the head waiter*) : What does all this
mean ?

THE HEAD WAITER : Your servant is right, mein
Herr.   There will be a festival here to-night,
and of a unique sort.   The *Fortschrittsverein*
students have honoured us in selecting this
place for their initiation ceremonies.   The
younger members, called *Foxes*, will be raised

---

[a] An initiation festival and drinking bout of the German
students.

to the rank of *Wolves*. As a rare exception, the *habitués* of the Brewery, known as Philistines, will be admitted to this celebration; but they can only occupy the second row of tables, outside the space reserved for the *Fortschrittsverein*. This place is for the great Schwartz, president of the *verein*. That keg of beer, upon which stands the jolly-looking bust of Gambrinus, is especially for him, and you will see him empty it before the evening is over. Just look at his glass, and judge of his stomach. They say that the Count von Bismarck is the only one who can compete with him. Last year a daring Bavarian challenged him to a drinking-bout, but rolled off his chair, dead drunk, after the tenth glass. Schwartz himself, although he had drunk twelve glasses, carried him on his shoulders to bed. Listen to the music of the *verein*. That big blond chap, with a silk scarf like the burgomaster's, who is walking behind the flag, that is Schwartz. The students follow in double file. The Philistines can be easily distinguished from those with coloured caps, corded jackets, and big boots. They are the old members, the *Wolves*. The *Foxes* wear a roundabout coat and a green cap. But I must be off to my work. Hurry and take a good place, for they will soon fill up; and I promise you you will not regret your evening.

*The tables fill rapidly. The* STUDENTS *arrive, preceded by a band of music.* SCHWARTZ *stops at his place. The* WOLVES *occupy the first row of tables, forming a semicircle. The* FOXES *remain standing, to wait upon the* WOLVES. *Among the* PHILISTINES, *in the outer row of tables, sits* TRÜBE, *trying to conceal his face with his hand; at another is* HERZ, *the Socialist, and* FLITZ, *with* ARISTIDES *standing behind his chair.*

SCHWARTZ (*raising his sword, and in a solemn voice*): Honour to Gambrinus! May his golden blessings ever flow in copious streams down the thirsty throats of the *Fortschrittsverein!* Approach, ye weasel-headed *Foxes!* As the first part of your initiation I must present you to Gambrinus, whom you must worship fervently. By Jupiter! you cannot drink beer with the same hand, or in the same spirit, as water. Beer is a living drink.

> " For beer was made to drink,
> And water to sail boats in."

The mild but violent spirit, sometimes foolish, more often clever, that Gambrinus has hidden in the molecules of beer, knows all the weak spots of heart and head. This spirit loves smoke—all kinds of smoke. Gambrinus and Rauch—beer and smoke—are above all other gods to a good *Wolf*. They introduce us to woman, and, combined with her, form the sacred trilogy of the college where the students know more than the professors. Here, Foxes, some beer !

*The* Foxes *fill the* Wolves' *glasses.* Schwartz *fills his own immense glass from the keg. He gives a haughty look around, while the* Wolves *beat time on the tables with their full glasses.* Schwartz *suddenly lifts his glass, and empties it quickly; as he finishes he strikes the table with his sword and shouts,* Paf !

Chorus of Students : Paf !

*They empty their glasses, and seizing the* Foxes, *who have not yet drunk, mockingly wipe their mouths with their caps.*

Schwartz (*raises his sword and sings*) :

> A student once there lived,
> Thrice foolish fellow, he

Would neither drink nor smoke,
Nor love the fair Houri.

Death, passing by that way,
Said, "Now, can this be so;
I'll ask my good old pal
To take this chap below."

A student who would live
Long time, and merry be,
Must quaff his beer, and smoke,
And love the fair Houri.

When Death shall pass that way,
This student need not fret;
Old Death will be so pleased
His mission he'll forget.

With drink, and smoke, and song,
And the love of the fair Houri,
We'll journey on through life,
And surely happy be.

   Hurrah! hurrah! hurrah!
   We'll surely happy be.

   *Chorus of* STUDENTS:

With drink and smoke and song,
And the love of the fair Houri,

We'll journey on through life,
And surely happy be.
 Hurrah! hurrah! hurrah!
 We'll surely happy be.

A STUDENT: Your poetry is not very racy,
 Schwartz. I prefer the old song.

  Gaudeamus igitur
  Juvenes dum sumus;
  Post exactam juventutem,
  Post molestam senectutem,
  Nos habebit humus.
  Vivat Academia!
  Vivant professores!
  Vivant omnes virgines
  Faciles accessu,
  Vivant et mulieres
  Faciles aggressu!

   *Chorus of* STUDENTS:

  Vivant mulieres et virgines.
  Faciles aggressu!

SCHWARTZ (*animated*):
  Fun and frolic, beer and wine;
  Beauty, joy, and youth divine;
   For ever and for aye!

Noise and racket, loud and long,
Kisses sweet and passions strong,
    For ever and for aye !

Wise men's sayings never mind,
These must all be left behind,
    For ever and for aye !

Listen, friends, as I unfold
This good maxim, ages old,
All that glitters is not gold,
    For ever and for aye !

*Chorus of* STUDENTS :

Listen, friends, as we unfold,
This good maxim, ages old,
All that glitters is not gold,
    For ever and for aye !

SCHWARTZ (*raising his sword*) : Now, Green-caps,
  approach.   Who are you ?
ONE OF THE FOXES : A *Fox*.
SCHWARTZ : What do you wish ?
THE FOX : The initiation of a German student.
SCHWARTZ : What else ?
THE FOX : To become a *Wolf*, a glorious *Wolf* of
  the *Fortschrittsverein*.

SCHWARTZ: Well said, Master Fox. Be a *Wolf*. Be honest, be faithful, be true. As Gambrinus must be worshipped, so must woman be loved; but most of all, at your country's call, be eager, ready, and willing.

SCHWARTZ *takes the* STUDENT'S *green cap, pierces it with his sword, then pours the contents of his beer-glass over the* STUDENT'S *head. The same ceremony is gone through with each* Fox.

ARISTIDES (*to Flitz*): These is mighty queer goin's on, massa. Coloured folks don't do like dat. Well, I should die laughing. Wasting all dat beer!

FLITZ: Shut up!

HERZ: The negro is right in ridiculing the white man.

TRÜBE (*to Flitz*): My dear sir, it is better to do such things when young, than when old. Erasmus was right in his praise of Folly. The world would be very dull, were we all like Socrates and Lucretia.

FLITZ: That, mein Herr, is a state of affairs we need not dread, either in the old world or the new.

SCHWARTZ (*brandishing his sword*): *Silentium!*

*The* FOXES *approach, and each, in turn, removes his cap from* SCHWARTZ'S *sword, on which it has been impaled.* The STUDENTS *repeat the chorus :* " *Gaudeamus igitur,*" *&c., &c. At a signal from* DR. FÜRST, *a curtain is drawn aside, revealing* "*Germania Victrix,*" *crowned with laurels, her right hand holding aloft a sword. At sight of this the students' enthusiasm turns into frenzy.*

### A STUDENT :

Our country calls for succour,
Make ready for the fray ;
To sisters, wives, and sweethearts
Your tender farewells say.
Germania's bone and sinew,
Her brightest and her best,
Shall crush the Danish tyrant,
And rescue the oppress'd.

### *Chorus of* STUDENTS :

We'll crush the Danish tyrant,
And rescue the oppress'd.

### *Another* STUDENT :

For some time past, since by the force of arms,
Our enemies were made to bite the dust,

All Germany has slept in sweet repose,
And dream'd but peaceful, quiet, happy dreams.
Who is it now disturbs this grateful rest,
A quarrel seeking ?  Come !  From East to West,
From Southern Alps to Northern Baltic's shores,
Brothers arise, and gird your armour on !
The German flag, with victor's laurels crown'd,
Shall make all Europe trembling, bow and kneel.

*Chorus of* STUDENTS :

The German flag with victor's laurels crown'd,
Shall make all Europe trembling, bow and kneel.

SCHWARTZ : I notice among the audience good
Dr. Fürst, who is always present when a
patriotic speech is to be made, and good beer
to be had.  Most worthy Doctor, our young
Foxes, who are not as yet acquainted with you,
will drink of the sacred spring of your elo-
quence with all the more gusto, as they have
already had enough of that of Gambrinus ; besides, it will do them good to hear a little *good*
oratory.  Venerable scholar, shining light of
the University of Berlin, you have the floor !

DR. FÜRST : Brother Germans, what is Germany?
It does not consist only of a number of provinces—now uuhappily at swords' points—

ruled by German princes. It is everywhere, where the German tongue is spoken, and where German hearts beat. There are, to-day fragments of the great but unhappy Germania in Switzerland, in Holland, in France, in Russia; but, recently, there were still some in Denmark. In time, and by God's help, the sword of Germany will rectify the geography of Europe. It will be a hard task; but Prussia, as the first and invincible worker, can accomplish it. The noble house of Hohenzollern has already begun the fulfilment of its historic mission, in freeing the Duchies from the Danish yoke. Who shall dare to oppose this grand undertaking? German science has opened the gates; it has surrounded with a halo the rights conferred upon the German nation, by the international treaties and by ethnology. It has exposed our grievances, suffered at the hands of our ambitious neighbours, who, profiting by our internal dissensions, have for centuries oppressed and harassed our sacred soil. In 1815 we taught the *Erb-feind* [4] a good lesson, and gave to Europe a

---

[4] Erbfeind; *Anglicè*, the hereditary enemy. The German nickname for the French.

startling proof of our strength in overthrowing Napoleon, and occupying his capital. But how many injuries are still unavenged? Who can forget Conradin von Hohenstauffen, and his execution by the French at Naples in 1268?

FLITZ: Oh! oh! That is very old! Do you happen to be his brother?

(*Groans in the audience.*)

FÜRST: I am the brother of all German victims to foreign tyranny. I am a brother to all the inhabitants of the Palatinate, destroyed by Turenne and the French, under Louis XIV. I am a brother to every German still groaning under foreign rule; the people of Alsace and Lorraine; the Swiss of Bern, Zurich, and Neuchâtel; the Teutons of the Baltic provinces; these belong to the German race; in their veins still flows the blood of that noble-hearted Herrmann, against whom the Gallo-Roman legions of Varus fought so ineffectually.

*Loud and long applause from the* STUDENTS, *who now resume their drinking.* FÜRST *seats himself at the table next to* FLITZ.

FLITZ (*to* FÜRST): Will you allow me, most worthy Doctor, to tell you a thought that occurred to

me during your eloquent discourse ? My great
grandfather was a French refugee. He married
a Prussian in Berlin. My father is a German,
naturalized American; my mother was Polish,
from Warsaw, consequently a Sclav. Without
going back any further—for during centuries
past the Germans, under the name of Goths,
Visigoths, Ostrogoths, Burguignians, Scythes,
or Franks have emigrated, armed and unarmed,
to the South and West, to Italy, Gaul, and
elsewhere—without referring to this, I ask, do
you really believe it possible for the most eru-
dite scholar, with the aid of his most powerful
magnifying-glass, to distinguish German blood
from the Italian, the Sclav, or the French ?
Let two nurses bring you two new-born infants,
one from Baden, the other from Nancy; could
you tell the difference between them, any more
than you could between two drops of water ?
If the nurses had exchanged the children,
would you feel able to rectify the mistake ?
I have an idea that when the Almighty organized the fusion of races, He allowed us to
ridicule a little bit ethnological science; at
least when it passes certain limits, and when
its doubtful deductions upon a lot of pro-

blematic races may result in the actual shedding of human blood. By what right do you wish to separate what God has so well mixed? Why provoke dissensions then, where His best workman, Time, has passed the summit? Keep your ethnology, mein Herr, for a time and place where it may prove useful; that is, as a landmark for your study; and don't throw it, as a firebrand, in the midst of explosive elements, of which there are only too many. Humanity—it is a pity that a Philistine should remind you of it—humanity is *the* supreme science; and all the others must bow down before it.

A DEMOCRAT: By your leave, I will add that Charlemagne, the great Emperor of the West, governed equally the Franks and Germans. Why should we not now, as then, form a single family? The French, descendants of the Franks or Gauls, are simply our German antecedents there.

FÜRST: I admire your lofty ideas of humanity, gentlemen—more especially in you, my American friend, as we have seen during your present civil war what little weight humanitarian theories and the principles of liberty and independence have with your statesmen when their political interests are at stake. And you, who, I fancy, pretend to be a partisan of the abolition of slavery, what are you doing with this negro ?

FLITZ: He is as free as you or I. Ask him yourself.

ARISTIDES: Yes, sah ! I'm free. Massa says so.

SCHWARTZ (*who has been listening*) : The negro is free. Bring him here.

ARISTIDES : Shall I go, massa ?

FLITZ : Certainly.

ARISTIDES *steps forward. The* STUDENTS *crown him with wreaths of flowers, and repeat over him the ceremony of initiation.* ARISTIDES *is delighted, and keeps repeating,* Yes, sah ! I'm free, just as free as white man !

HERZ (*to* FLITZ) : I congratulate you, mein Herr, on your courageous frankness. Our hearts beat just as hard for Germany as this cursed Doctor's; but we know too well, the danger threatening domestic amelioration and liberty, when foreign politics of an aggressive nature are made a part of our national education. This ambition and hatred, which are for ever being drummed into the German mind, these everlasting incentives to military glory and conquering patriotism can blind the young nobility; but for us, workmen, mechanics, merchants, it makes us distrustful. We only ask for peace, a cessation of feudal abuses, a fair assessment of taxes, and an equal distribution of justice; for in this we fear some trickery, that the hobbies of a few may be gratified. We are good patriots, but we do not wish to be made dupes!

FLITZ: I understand you thoroughly, my friend; but, do what you may, I fear you will yet for a long time be dupes. (*Pointing to the* STUDENTS.) See how they enjoy themselves. Now, let us listen to Fürst.

FÜRST: A true and lasting peace in Europe can not be until Germany shall have accomplished her historic task, when all the scattered branches shall be attached to the old Germanic trunk. Germany must be satiated before Europe can rest in peace. Until then, Germany must fulfil her mission of civilization,[5] waving aloft her naked sword; and she will not cease enforcing her demands till she has securely laid the foundation of her glory, and made universal peace an accomplished fact.

[5] Kulturkampf.

E

FLITZ: Decidedly, Doctor Fürst is a plagiarist; Alexander, Cæsar, Napoleon, and, if I mistake not, Attila, always said the same thing, almost the same words, in their respective languages. It is always for "just demands" and "universal peace" that the great human butchers have disturbed all peace, and caused rivers of blood to flow.

(*Exeunt* FLITZ *and* HERZ.)

LOREMBERG (*to* TRÜBE): Never, your Excellency, until to-day have I thoroughly appreciated the wisdom of our rulers. Where should we be if our good king, through such faithful allies as Fürst and other university professors, did not direct against foreign interests the flood of generous passions and the bursts of anger with which the youthful German heart is bubbling over? What power could resist this torrent, if, instead of having as objective the just demands of our patriotism, it should take the fatal direction chosen by the democrat-socialists?

TRÜBE: You are perfectly right, mein Herr.

*The* STUDENTS *have formed a circle around* ARISTIDES, *who is dressed in the discarded cap and jacket of a* FOX. *The* STUDENTS *dance around him, singing and shouting.*

ARISTIDES (*very much excited and dancing with the others*) : Hooray ! Germany's a bully place; must have war to have peace; must fight for civilization; Hooray !

*Two* STUDENTS *begin to dispute, and end in a quarrel, which becomes general. Glasses go whizzing through the air; chairs are broken; swords are drawn; many* STUDENTS *are already under the tables, dead drunk; the rest are fighting. The patrol arrives and arrests the combatants, who go off singing—*

> Vivant virgines et mulieres,
> Faciles aggressu !

### FIFTH TABLEAU.

*The Prelude to the Austro-Prussian War.*

### SCENE XIV.

*Bismarck's Private Study.*

*The* KING *and* BISMARCK.

BISMARCK : Well, sire, it is agreed. You go to Gastein. The Emperor of Austria will be there, and you will settle the affair about in these terms : Prussia and Austria will share the ad-

E 2

ministration of the Duchies; Holstein goes to
our allies; Schleswig to us. Europe will
clamour against Austria and Prussia; we will
let them clamour. It is better that the Austrian
Government should be compromised in this
affair as much as possible, so that *its* action
shall be criticized when occasion offers. This
little treaty, sire, binds us to nothing, and
leaves everything possible for the future; it is
purely imaginary. The main point is not to
excite before the proper time our ally's susceptibilities, and the defiance of the minor states.

THE KING: Exactly. And you, Herr Graf, where
are you going during my absence?

BISMARCK: I had thought somewhat, your majesty,
of going to Varzin, but my physician has
ordered me to Biarritz.

THE KING: Biarritz!

BISMARCK: Yes.

THE KING: Ah! And what are you going to say
to Napoleon?

BISMARCK: Oh! I shall amuse him—try to find
out his plans, and tell him ours.

THE KING: Tell him ours?

BISMARCK: That is the surest way to prevent his
finding them out.

THE KING: Be careful, Herr Graf, that you promise nothing.

BISMARCK: That would not matter much. But there is no need for such promises. These French are so conceited, and so willing to believe what they think.

THE KING: I fancy my good brother, Napoleon, is growing old. He lacks the energy and cunning of days gone by.

BISMARCK: He certainly, sire, seems fifty years older than your majesty, though actually ten years younger.

THE KING: Then he has reached his second childhood?

BISMARCK: I am so convinced of this that I think I shall advise him to take Belgium.

THE KING: Do you mean it?

BISMARCK: Rest assured, sire, there will be nothing in black and white.

THE KING: But why this advice? Suppose he should follow it?

BISMARCK: All the better! We should then be free to do and dare—everything. But he knows too well the distrust he inspires in all Europe, and he will dare do nothing. He will simply listen to me; and that, perhaps, will some of these days suffice to estrange England from him.

THE KING: I begin to see that your idea is not a bad one. Any news from Vienna since yesterday?

BISMARCK: Yes, sire; Captain Walter, whom I sent there, has returned with a most interesting budget of news, a condensed report of which will shortly be handed you. Captain Walter is an officer of merit who must be advanced. He is very zealous in your service, sire; and, during the war of the Duchies, furnished us with much useful information. Your Majesty would do well to take him to Gastein.

THE KING: Willingly. You will send him to me.

(*Exit the* KING.)

## SCENE XV.

### BISMARCK *and* WALTER.

BISMARCK (*to a* SERVANT): Show in Captain Walter. (*Enter* WALTER.) Captain, I am happy to inform you that, on my recommendation, his majesty has chosen you to accompany him to Gastein, where he is to have an interview with the Emperor of Austria.

WALTER: I had cherished a hope that I should be sent to Paris; but as his majesty and yourself have decided otherwise, I am ready.

BISMARCK: I was very much pleased with your reports from Copenhagen and Vienna; I hope to be equally so with those from Gastein. Send me every day news of his majesty's precious health.

WALTER: Every day, Herr Graf.

BISMARCK: Be on the most cordial terms with the Austrian officers. Dissensions often arise from too slight an acquaintance.

WALTER: You will always find me ready, willing and devoted, Herr Graf; for none more than I have at heart the glory and honour of Germany.

BISMARCK: I know that, captain; for that reason have I chosen you. You are anxious for a mission to France, eh? Well, you shall go to Paris as military attaché of legation when —when we shall have arranged this little difficulty with Austria.

(WALTER *bows and exit.*)

## SIXTH TABLEAU.

### SCENE XVI.

*The* WALTERS' *sitting-room, as in the first tableau.*
WILHELMINE *and* PETRUS WALTER.

WILHELMINE: Victory, Petrus!

WALTER: You have news from Paris?

WILHELMINE: Hear! The Montalbans accept
our invitation for August at our villa at En-
ghien. You understand—you can make love at
your leisure under the trees and on the shores
of the lake. You love each other, the father
consents, and this winter you will return to
Berlin with a lovely bride.

WALTER: Ah! my dear sister; it really seems as
if a fatality were ever pursuing me. At any
other time, this letter you show me would have
made me the happiest of men. Well—it will
be absolutely impossible for me to be in Paris
during August; at that time I shall be in
attendance upon the king at Gastein. I have
just received my orders from Count von Bismarck.

WILHELMINE: It is an opportunity missed, Petrus;
let us hope it is not an opportunity lost.

# ACT II.

## Dramatis Personæ.

Dr. Johnson ⎱ *In the Audience.*
Jean Durand ⎰

King William I.

Count von Bismarck.

Field-Marshal von Moltke.

General Herzog.

M. Benedetti, *Ambassador of France.*

Field-Marshall von Manteuffel.

Wagner, *Socialist Deputy to the Landtag.*

Captain Petrus Walter.

Schwartz, *Lieutenant in the Landwehr.*

Loremberg, *the Jewish Banker.*

The Burgomaster of Frankfort.

The Notables of Frankfort.

Fritz, *Soldier of the Landwehr.*

Maria, *his Wife.*

Frau Walter,

Johann Goschen, *an Invalid Artilleryman.*

Flora, *his Sister.*

## FIRST TABLEAU.

*The War against Austria.*

### SCENE I.

SCENE : *A garden.* FLORA *and* LOREMBERG
*walking together.*

DURAND : I think, doctor, that I recognize this
young woman. Is it not Flora?

JOHNSON : Certainly.

DURAND : It is she; and yet it is not. Her
features have not changed, but her expression
does not appear to be the same.

JOHNSON : The face tells the story of her life.
Flora, thanks to this old Jew's protection, has
become a countess or baroness—what shall I
say—over the left. She is now the mistress
of Trübe, one of the hidden powers of the day.
Being at once clever and unscrupulous, she
has, at one step, risen from obscurity to the
secrets of diplomacy. In Berlin, where she
would be too quickly recognized, she keeps
carefully in the background; but in Florence,
Vienna, and Paris, she has been introduced
into several salons as Baroness de Vinzenan,

and has been thoroughly appreciated and approved of by the Count for services rendered. In return for the position obtained for her by this old Jew, she uses her influence in the high places for the benefit of his financial enterprises. So goes the world in virtuous Germany.

LOREMBERG (*to Flora*): You are back, dear Baroness, and pleased with your stay in Paris?

FLORA: Yes, and I agree with those who say there is no place like Paris. Ah! the Count may ease his mind. No matter what happens, he will not cause the French to miss one moment's enjoyment, or one joke. It only needed the sight of their gaiety (not like our gaiety, stupid and serious,) to reconcile me to myself. Oh! jolly and vicious people. (*Assuming a serious tone.*) But I ask myself, Loremberg, if French vices are not better than our virtues?

LOREMBERG: I congratulate you, Baroness, on the improved morals you bring with you from France.

FLORA: Ah, Loremberg, why have you waited so long to preach morals to me?

LOREMBERG (*laughing*) : Well said, my dear child ; you are much more clever than I.

FLORA : That is just what the King of Italy said to me last winter.

LOREMBERG : Really ! And how did you find this King with the big moustache ?

FLORA : Charming ; although rather too " go-ahead." He would much rather make love than talk politics. It is, at any rate, evident that the Count can rely upon—if not the King himself, at least his faithful subjects, even though he should carry the war into France. For the Italians owe too much to the French not to hate them cordially ; besides, they take no pains to hide their feelings.

LOREMBERG : Did you see Garibaldi ?

FLORA : Yes ; I was for eight days at Caprera.

LOREMBERG : Ah !

FLORA : And I shouted " *Viva l'Italia* " so well with him, that he wanted to marry me.

LOREMBERG : Heroes have their weak moments as well as—

FLORA : Bankers and diplomats, I suppose you would say ?

LOREMBERG : That is about it. Did you suggest to Garibaldi what glory and honour he could obtain, if, in case of war between Prussia and Austria, he should make a raid on Dalmatia ?

FLORA: Of course. He would have started at once, had I only said the word. Believe me, Loremberg, heroes are the biggest fools of all.

LOREMBURG: What a wonderful diplomat you have become, fair Baroness ! The Count will be delighted to hear these things from your own lips; he will see that I did not overrate your spirit of observation. Don't forget to put in a little word for me about the next war loan. You know when I am rubbed the right way I am not ungrateful. (*Some noise is heard.*) Ah ! here is the Count; but the King is with him. Let us get out of the way.

## SCENE II.

### *The* KING *and* BISMARCK.

THE KING: The time has come, Herr Graf. Germany is no longer big enough for Prussia and Austria. One of the two must yield her place to the other. With the help of God and my good army, I hope it will not be Prussia.

BISMARCK: Of that I am certain, sire.

THE KING: Von Moltke promises victory, and

a rapid one, thanks to our admirable army organization and the *dis*-organization of the enemy. The question is, who will the Austrians have for allies ?

BISMARCK: Nobody, sire. If you desire proof, will your majesty hear this despatch just received from Herr von Goltz, in Paris (*reads*) : " From reliable sources, I learn that Italy says, Prussia is seeking her aid in a war against the common enemy, Austria. Italy, desirous only of the freedom of Venetia, prefers to attain her point, rather by an amicable arrangement with Austria, France acting as intermediary, than by an alliance with Prussia. Italy asks the Emperor's advice."

THE KING : Ah, we shall see what Napoleon says !

BISMARCK (*reads*) : " The Emperor advises Italy to accept our propositions."

THE KING (*astonished*) : Ah, Bismarck, what a charming fellow is this French emperor !

BISMARCK : We should indeed do well to be grateful to him. Napoleon thinks Austria strong and Prussia weak. Leaving this aside, his foresight is perfect and his policy admirably clever.

THE KING : Decidedly, Herr Graf, your two sea-
sons at Biarritz have not been without their
fruits.

BISMARCK : You may be sure, sire, my words are
still ringing in his ears.' I bewildered him
with the audacity of my propositions. I ex-
tolled Cavour to him incessantly, and more
than once hinted at the *Piedmontese Mission* of
Prussia. I thought it well to have his mind
thoroughly imbued with this idea, inasmuch as
he is doubtful of our strength, and only sees in
our projects a means of crushing his enemies
and selling us his aid at a good figure, when
the occasion offers. He wanted me to make
him direct offers. I did. I offered him—
Belgium ! For the rest I leave him to hope ;
but no promises that could ever be brought up
for fulfilment. I led him to believe that
Prussia is the natural ally of France.

THE KING : And this lord of Biarritz swallowed
all this ?

BISMARCK : He would have swallowed even more ;
for I pretended to admire his profound silence,
whereas I really laughed more than he at my
own babble. He evidently thought me very
innocent ; he even told some one that I was

not earnest enough.  I should be very sorry to have him realize how much so I am.  The shores of Biarritz have heard some remarkable things wafted away by the mocking winds.  I praised France, and made fun of Prussia, ridiculing the big-wigs in the House of Lords and the prattlers in the Chamber of Deputies.  I did not even spare you, sire.  I complained of being in the service of a king too little ambitious, too honest, and of too domestic habits.  Seeing his persistent silence, I asked him, "Well, what would *you* care to have?"  To which he answered, with an innocent air of astonishment, "We! we want nothing!"

THE KING : Hypocrite!

BISMARCK: No matter.  He understood, or at least, thought he did; so we can start at once.

THE KING : And if, as I hope, the God of battles crowns our efforts, Napoleon will have learned to know Germany better by her actions than through her ambassadors.  You can cease your diplomatic manœuvres against the Viennese court.  It is now Von Moltke's turn. Here is the order of mobilization!

## SECOND TABLEAU.

*Off for the War.*

### SCENE III.

*The outside of a railway station in Berlin.* SOL-
DIERS *arriving from every quarter to join their
regiments.*

SCHWARTZ (*in the uniform of a lieutenant of Landwehr*) : Au revoir, my friends ! We shall have
a glorious feast at the *Fortschrittsverein* when
we return. We will drink a grand *salamander*[1]
for the missing ones. What happy times we
live in ! There is no longer a chance of dying
of *ennui* when other methods of dying are so
freely offered. Rejoice, O noble poet Geiber—
you who complained of the dangerous, suffo-
cating, corrupting peace by which the Germans
were for ever in civil strife. For some years
past we have scattered abroad this overflow of
life given us by Jove. It is a pity you ever

[1] When a student is buried, his brother students meet to
drink a *salamander* (*ein salamander reiben*). They rub
their glasses around on the table, to imitate the roll of
funeral drums ; at a signal, the glasses are all emptied at
one gulp, and then broken.

F

died, O poet! You could have heard the bullets whistling to your heart's content, yesterday in the Duchies, to-morrow in Austria, the next day—who knows? Well, we are off, and perhaps well off. The King and the Count have wonderfully fathomed German nature.

A STUDENT: Schwartz, let us have a few *schoppen* before we start.

SCHWARTZ: Did a German student ever refuse a few *schoppen*? (*They enter a beer saloon.*)

*Groups of* SOLDIERS, *accompanied by* WIVES *and* CHILDREN, *saying farewell.*

MARIA (*weeping*): Adieu, Fritz!

FRITZ: Au revoir, Maria.

MARIA: Write to me often.

FRITZ: As often as possible; and when I come back we shall be married.

MARIA: Ah! when you come back! How I shall pray for you!

JOHANN: Above all, Maria, pray to God, for a German victory.

MARIA: I shall rather pray God to fill the hearts of our German sovereigns with a love for peace.

JOHANN: That girl is a bad patriot!

FRITZ: Don't abuse her; she is a good honest girl, and what she says is true. It will not make me serve my country less well, though I fail to see what benefits will accrue to Germany from this victory.

JOHANN: Fool! Do you not see that, for Germany to retain her power and unity, she must thrash Austria and her German allies; that without this union is an impossibility; and, without a firmly-cemented union, some of these fine days the enemy will invade us again?

FRITZ: I believe it, since every one says the same thing; but, nevertheless, it is a pity that this noble aim cannot be realized without the shedding of so much German blood, and with the help of outsiders.

MARIA: Leave that infatuated fool, Fritz. I have but a few moments more with you, and you devote them to others. Come!

A MARRIED SOLDIER (*to an old man*): Thanks mein Herr, for your kind offers. I am truly grateful, but you cannot prevent my ruin. Less than six months ago I bought that little property. We scraped along, hoping much for the future. My wife, Martha, tired herself out with work and the care of the children.

War breaks out; our economies of ten years vanish in smoke. But what hurts still more is the thought of my poor wife's constant anxiety. Ah! if kings only knew what it costs to make war, there would be an everlasting peace. Ah! here is Martha, poor girl!

*Enter* MARTHA, *with her* CHILDREN. *They all take leave of their Father, weeping. Other scenes of this sort.*

JOHANN (*seated at the door of an inn*) : My friends, to the health of the King and the victory of Germany!

SCHWARTZ *and the* STUDENTS : Hurrah! hurrah!

(*Cheers for* KING WILLIAM, COUNT VON BISMARCK, *and Germany.*)

WAGNER (*rising, and with a solemn air*): I drink to Germany and German liberty!

JOHANN : Who is this?

A STUDENT: It is Wagner, a socialist and member of the Landtag.

WAGNER: Friends, let us wish success to the German arms; but let us also hope that this victory may not prove inimical to the development of our liberties, and that those in power shall not forget that even in the most just war the object aimed at must be the reign of justice and the establishing of a lasting peace.

*Voices from different parts of the audience:*
Bravo! bravo! No! no!

JOHANN: I don't like such restrictions when we are off for the war.

WAGNER: Friend Johann, you are brave; you have already paid your debt to your country. But bravery is not all in this world. We can never surpass the old-time barbarians in courage, but we can surpass them in humanity, in knowledge of the true and good, in a broader and more exalted idea of the human destiny. I fear our statesmen think very little of all this. In this present war I see princely rivalries, and an ambition for which German unity is rather the pretext than the true aim. The old Confederacy, with perhaps a few reforms, seems to me preferable to this union; and, further, once on the way by force of arms, where will we stop? With this idea the strongest heads are turned. That is how the people pay dearly for quarrels of the kings. I trust, brave Johann, that my presentiments may be wrong. I think we will conquer Austria, but beyond that I dare not look. To the

good health and long life of German common
sense! (*Drinks.*)

SCHWARTZ : Now that I have drunk, mein Herr,
allow me to remind you that you are not at the
tribunal of the Landtag, but on a public square.
Allow me also to quote from the Gospel:
"Sufficient unto the day is the evil thereof."
It seems to me that the present is serious
enough, without looking into the future.
There may be truth in what you say, but we
have plenty of time to think over it. Leave
serious affairs for to-morrow, for next year.
Come, my friends, forward! And with your
best voices give us a patriotic song!

*A regiment arrives, the band playing a patriotic
air. The crowd join in singing it, and follow
into the railway station.*

### THIRD TABLEAU.

*The battle of Sadowa—July 3rd, 1866.*

### SCENE IV.

*A height near Sadowa.*

BISMARCK, *wearing the uniform of a colonel of
cuirassiers;* GENERAL HERZOG ; CAPTAIN
WALTER. *All three on horseback.*

WALTER: Things are looking well for us, Herr Graf; so Field-Marshal von Moltke has just informed his Majesty.

BISMARCK: In effect, I believe that Marshal Benedek cannot long hold out against this unexpected concentration of our forces. Either I am very much mistaken or Austria as a great military power will not exist to-morrow. (*To* HERZOG.) General, nobody better than you perhaps can judge of the chances. Will you ascend that little hill, and let us know what you think and see?

HERZOG: Certainly, Herr Graf.


## SCENE V.

### BISMARCK *and* WALTER.


BISMARCK : Now, captain, let us profit of the few moments before his Majesty arrives. I find your report concerning Kings John of Saxony and Louis of Bavaria too laconic. Tell me, word for word, what you learned. You hear, captain, *word for word;* I wish it, no matter how uncomplimentary it may be either to his Majesty or to myself.

WALTER: Since you so desire, Herr Graf, here it is. You will understand in my frankness the sincerity of my devotion to the King, the future of Prussia, and yourself.

BISMARCK: Go on.

WALTER: After the usual compliments were passed, and after the interchange of their respective communications (which I forwarded to you in the most speedy manner possible), King Louis and King John gave their impressions on the situation. King John said, " After all, sire, I care no more for Prussia than for Austria, and should much prefer to remain neutral, but I consider Prussia much more dangerous for us if she gets the better of her rival." To which King Louis answered, " Those are precisely my sentiments, sire. What a sad fate is ours to have to choose between two hateful situations!" "Yes," answered King John; " for it all comes to this: shall we be eaten with a Prussian or an Austrian sauce?" " What do you foresee?" asked the King of Bavaria. " I dare foresee nothing," from King John. All of which, Herr Graf, I think, shows that neither of them for one moment doubted the success of our arms.

BISMARCK: Continue, captain; it is most interesting.

WALTER: "I have but little confidence in Benedek," said King Louis; "the Austrian army lacks cohesion; it is but poorly armed. As for our brave Federal troops, I only fear that Prussia will not give them a chance. Let us hope, however, God will favour the justice of our cause." "Leave God out of the question," quickly interrupted the King of Saxony; "If He thinks of us at all, it is only to pity us. He must once again regret that He created mankind when, on the one hand— (WALTER *hesitates*.)

BISMARCK: Speak out, captain; the more harsh the expressions the more I shall appreciate your frankness.

WALTER: —"When, on the one hand, He hears the mystical and blasphemous expressions of King William, and, on the other, He reads the perfidious and shameless despatches of Bismarck, who, having unchained the dogs of war, tries to make the world believe Francis Joseph the aggressor.

(BISMARCK *bursts out laughing*.)

BISMARCK: But go on, captain, this is delicious.

WALTER: " What do you think of Napoleon's policy ? " asked King Louis. To which King John: " He is as much a fool with his profound air of mysterious policy as Bismarck a knave."

BISMARCK (*laughing*): He said " knave," captain ?

WALTER: That is the word our agent heard. Pray excuse—

BISMARCK: But go on, go on, it is charming !

WALTER: " They are two thieves," added King John, " who, after having robbed their neighbour, fall to and cut each other's throats. Napoleon only sees danger on the Austrian side, and, moreover, hopes that the two states will wear each other out. He looks on with pleasure, and morally favours Prussia, only because he believes her to be weak, knowing full well that should he be in error he will still be the gainer, having got rid of his Venetian thorn in the side." " But," said King Louis, " that is not such poor reasoning." " Did you ever hear of Gribouille ? " asked King John, smiling. " If I remember rightly," answered King Louis, " he was a French character, who, wishing to get out of the rain jumped into the water." "It is the greatest power of the day," said the King of Saxony, "who is actually playing Gribouille. To escape a slight Italian wetting he plunges into a German torrent, which, after having absorbed us, will soon engulf him." "As for me," concluded King Louis, in a melancholy tone, "though I have only had a taste of kingly honours, I am tired of them. My ambition is more for perfecting the fine arts than for power. I would willingly give my kingdom to have composed an opera like Wagner's. I have already drawn the plans for a colossal theatre, where I can produce the music of the future." "Do not worry," said King John, "we are already beaten. You will have plenty of opportunities to study music and build theatres. I fancy that even the powers in Berlin will smile upon you, so long as you do not meddle with military music." The two kings then separated; the elder one very thoughtful, the younger one whistling an air from *Tannhäuser*.

BISMARCK: Thanks, captain. As a reward for your services, you will carry the official despatches to Her Majesty Queen Augusta, announcing the victory. When we return to

Berlin you shall go to Paris as military attaché to the German Legation.

WALTER: Herr Graf, you can count upon my eternal gratitude and devotion.

## SCENE VI.

*The same, the* KING *and* STAFF, GENERAL HERZOG *(all on horseback).*

THE KING: The God of battles has showered His blessings upon us, Herr Graf; Benedek abandons his positions. We have conquered. But what frightful carnage!

> *The* KING *motions to the* OFFICERS *to retire, and is left alone with* BISMARCK.

BISMARCK: Austria is beaten, sire. To-morrow , she must be put out of the Confederacy, and Prussia must be at the head of United Germany.

THE KING: What tears, lives, and misery to attain this grand result!

BISMARCK: All these are nought compared with the result obtained. Each year emigration takes away more of your subjects than ten battles of Sadowa.

THE KING : Emigration is not death.

BISMARCK : In a week your Majesty will be crowned at Vienna Emperor of Germany.

THE KING : I should now like to see the face made by my good brother, the Emperor of Austria.

BISMARCK : And I should like to see the face made by your good brother Napoleon, when he hears of this (by him) unlooked-for victory.

WAGNER (*one of the wounded, lying near, raises his head*) : Sire, one word; and you too, Herr Graff, draw near. I wish to make a revelation before I die.

THE KING : Do you know this poor fellow, Herr Graff?

BISMARCK : Yes; it is Wagner, formerly a Democratic deputy.

WAGNER : True, Herr Graff, I am a democrat. I am, above all, an enemy to ambition and false glory, which does not prevent my being killed for my country, even though its rights be doubtful. Have a care, sire; you are on a dangerous road, from which we tried to save you when we voted against your military organization. Remember to what fatal effects

the same causes led the first Napoleon ! I
heard your last words. I can tell you what
you would find more interesting than the faces
of the two Emperors; the faces of the fathers,
mothers, brothers, sisters, children, sweethearts
or wives of these poor devils, from whom the
vain pomp and glory of your pride—our
national pride, if you will—have ravished all
support, all happiness, and all hope.

(WAGNER *falls back, dead.   The* KING *seems
moved.*)

BISMARCK : That is the shortest speech he ever
made.   One babbler the less in the Landtag.

THE KING (*severely*) : Perhaps ; but one gallant
soldier the less in my army. (*A scout arrives,
bearing a despatch to the King.*)   Moltke sends
word that the enemy are in full retreat, leaving
behind arms and baggage.   The victory is still
more thorough than at first sight.   Unfortunately, the number of killed and wounded is
also greater than by first accounts.   There are
many sick ; several cases of cholera have
appeared.

BISMARCK : None of these things, sire, need stop
our advance.   We must push the victory on

to the end. To give the vanquished a chance to reconnoitre, to argue, with an enemy when we can crush him, would be as unpardonable a mistake in the General-in-Chief as in the ' Prime Minister.

THE KING : But, Herr Graff, I keep wondering if a less violent as well as a more Christian policy would not create a better impression in Europe.

BISMARCK : The most Christian policy, sire, is that, the results of which are the most assured, the most lasting—the prevention of new wars. Austria must be annihilated, all Germany brought under our laws; or else, later on, we shall have to begin all over again.

THE KING : You have already so well aided Providence to carry out her designs for Prussia, that I cannot but give heed to your counsels.

AN OFFICER (*saluting*): M. Benedetti, the French Ambassador, has just arrived at the General's headquarters. He begs leave to speak to your Majesty.

BISMARCK : Benedetti here ! What can he want ?

## Scene VII.

### *The same,* M. Benedetti.

BENEDETTI : Accept my congratulations, sire.

THE KING : With many thanks, your Excellency.

BISMARCK : His Majesty the Emperor will be rejoiced to hear of our success.

BENEDETTI : As much so as he will be grieved to hear some bad news just received from Italy.

THE KING AND BISMARCK : What bad news, Excellency ?

BENEDETTI : Have you not heard that the Archduke Albert has beaten the Italians at Custozza; and that Admiral Tegethoff has destroyed Persano's fleet at Lissa ? [2]

THE KING : I learn with sorrow of this mishap to our gallant allies.

BISMARCK : Victors or vanquished, by their timely diversion they have helped us to inflict upon Austria a defeat from which she can never recover.   In a week we shall be in Vienna.

[2] So far, the author has kept strictly to historic truths. But in this act he seems to have allowed himself a poet's licence.   For—without speaking of the improbability of M. Benedetti's appearance at the battle of Sadowa—the battle of Custozza took place on the 24th of June, and the naval engagement at Lissa, the 28th of July.—EDITOR.

BENEDETTI : What ! such a victory does not satisfy you ? You wish to enter Vienna ?

BISMARCK : Without a doubt.

BENEDETTI : I beg of you, sire, and of you also, Herr Graff, to see in me not only the Ambassador of France; but a friend, a sincere friend, who has already given you strong proofs of his friendship, and who now would emphasise these proofs by stronger ones. Here is a piece of news I had not yet told you. The Emperor Francis Joseph has telegraphed to the Emperor Napoleon, giving him Venetia. My Imperial master has immediately handed it over to King Victor Emanuel.

THE KING : There is nothing astonishing in this proceeding of my good brother of Austria. But his determination was taken too late; it cannot break our alliance with Italy.

BENEDETTI : It is possible, sire; but—remember, I am speaking as a friend, not as an ambassador—this event changes entirely the situation of France. The French government will be grateful to you for helping to carry out the imperial programme of 1859 ; but it is evident that Venetia, once given back to Italy, it cannot look upon your successes with such sympathetic interest. You can understand, that should you insist upon occupying Vienna, the national sentiment of the French people would exact from the Imperial government a totally different policy, if the government itself did not take the initiative.

BISMARCK: The national sentiment of the French people! As there is no ambassador here, only a friend, look at me without laughing, M. Benedetti.

BENEDETTI: That would be hard work, Herr Graf, when I think of all you said and wrote about the national sentiment of the German people, when you wanted to make war against Austria.

(BISMARCK *wishes to answer. The* KING *stops him.*)

THE KING: That is sufficient, Excellency—I forgot ... *M. Benedetti.* We only half understand each other. Such grave problems are not solved in a moment. You will thank our well-loved brother, Napoleon, for his kind sympathy, and assure him of ours.

BISMARCK: Say that we can never forget the proofs of his sincere sympathy, especially the one of which you have just been the interpreter.

BENEDETTI : I will transmit, sire, to my imperial sovereign, the expression of your good wishes.

(*Bows and exit.*)

## SCENE VIII.

### *The* KING *and* BISMARCK.

THE KING : Well, Herr Graff, what do you say ?

BISMARCK : Napoleon is trying on a little game, which—we should have expected.

THE KING : And for which he shall be made to pay.

BISMARCK : Oh ! as for that it is as good as paid ; for now, Austria beaten, we need not fear France. The only question is, whether we had better act at once, or wait a little time to give Napoleon this lesson he so well deserves ?

THE KING : What do you think ?

BISMARCK : It might do at once, but it would be better to be *sure.* We can decide nothing without consulting the field-marshal. Ah ! here he comes, at last.

## SCENE IX.

### *The* KING, BISMARCK, VON MOLTKE.

THE KING (*to Von Moltke*) : I congratulate you,

General. You have gloriously commanded the gallant army which has crushed the military power of Austria, and which has placed Prussia in her proper rank, in Germany and in Europe.

MOLTKE: The greatest praise, sire, is due to your wisdom, your courageous decisions, and the admirable bravery of your soldiers.

THE KING: Let us give thanks to the God of battles, without whose aid, my wisdom and your strategy would have gone for nought. A serious event has occurred here, while you were completing Benedek's defeat. The French ambassador has given us to understand that Napoleon cannot continue his friendly neutrality, if we push things any further. If we enter Vienna, it is war with France. Are we in a condition to undertake it?

MOLTKE (*after a moment's thought*): I think we are, sire. We have a large army excited with victory. The Dreyse gun, of which you have seen the wonderful effects, makes each one of our soldiers equal to four. Besides, our enemy is in trouble in Mexico; I *know* that his army is more disorganized than he imagines; and I am convinced he will be beaten. But in three or four years all the more surely, when we shall have introduced into our army some changes for the better, suggested by the present campaign; and when your diplomacy shall have culled from this victory the fruits it must bear, and enlisted immediately in our service the forces of the smaller conquered states.

BISMARCK : I have notified the official representatives of Baden, Wurtemberg, Saxony, and Bavaria. They know already with what a heavy hand we strike, and they will find it still heavier, unless an alliance, offensive and defensive, is signed without delay, and their entire military force placed in our hands. As for the King of Hanover, the Elector of Hesse, the Duke of Nassau, we are forced and authorized by all kinds of reasons, simply to unite their respective provinces to the Kingdom of Prussia.

THE KING : Praise be to the Almighty, who has chosen me as the glorious instrument to carry out His designs in Germany! It is His high Providence, which forces me, notwithstanding my unwillingness, to take the crown from my beloved brothers the King of Hanover, the

Duke of Nassau, the Elector of Hesse; to humiliate Darmstadt, Baden, Saxony, Bavaria, and Wurtemberg.

BISMARCK: Sire, you have not mentioned the Hanseatic towns; and above all Frankfort. The Providence which watches over Germany inspired the follies of the citizens of Frankfort, to oblige your Majesty to take this ancient imperial city.

THE KING: You think so, Herr Graf?

BISMARCK: I am sure of it.

THE KING: God's will be done! Can man do anything against the inscrutable decrees of Providence?

## FOURTH TABLEAU.

*The Prussians in Frankfort.*

### SCENE X.

*The Kaisersaal in the Rœmer Palace. The* BURGOMASTER *and the* NOTABLES *of Frankfort.*

THE BURGOMASTER: Meine Herren, I have called you together by order of the new Prussian commandant, whose communications we are now awaiting. This is all I am at liberty to say, in the unhappy state of the country.

A NOTABLE: The bird of prey [3] has, then, actually gone ?

THE BURGOMASTER: Yes, but he cost us dear. The two-and-twenty days of Prussian occupation, under his orders, have so bled the good city of Frankfort, that it will take at least ten years to recuperate.

FIRST NOTABLE: Sixty thousand pairs of shoes !

SECOND NOTABLE: Three hundred horses !

THIRD NOTABLE: Two hundred carriages !

THE BURGOMASTER: And six million florins counted out to him this very morning before his departure. Decidedly, we must change the proverb about him who works for the King of Prussia.

FIRST NOTABLE: Happily, all requisitions are ended. The bird of prey gave his formal word of honour.

SECOND NOTABLE: The word of a thief !

THIRD NOTABLE: Silence !

SECOND NOTABLE: A Prussian officer said yesterday at my house that if the Socialist writer,

---

[3] A pun on the name of General *Vogel der Falkenstein*, whom the citizens of Frankfort nicknamed *Vogel der Raubenstein*.

Sonnemann, was not given up, we should soon be assessed for a new war contribution.

FIRST NOTABLE (*to the* BURGOMASTER): Did you tell the bird of prey, Herr Burgomaster, that the Republic of Frankfort was not at war with Prussia, and that the conduct of the latter was contrary to all human right?

THE BURGOMASTER: That is the first thing I told him. He answered, that might made human right; that the population of Frankfort was renowned for its enmity and hatred of Prussia; and that it was necessary, for the safety of Germany, to give Frankfort an exemplary chastisement.

FIRST NOTABLE: Hypocrites! It is for the safety of Germany that they insult, rob, and kill so many honest Germans!

THE BURGOMASTER: Meine Herren, the Field-Marshal von Manteuffel!

## SCENE XI.

*The same,* MANTEUFFEL, *in full uniform, and followed by his staff.*

MANTEUFFEL: Meine Herren, I have summoned you to inform you that the city of Frankfort is assessed for a war contribution of twenty-five million florins, payable in twenty four hours.

OMNES: Twenty-five millions!

MANTEUFFEL: Yes, twenty-five millions.

THE BURGOMASTER: Most worthy sir, you are doubtless unaware that your honourable predecessor, General von Falkenstein, has already levied six million florins, besides innumerable requisitions of other kinds; that this amount, paid to him this morning, was only raised by bleeding the city of Frankfort at every pore.

MANTEUFFEL: General von Falkenstein did but obey his orders. I must do likewise. I know I shall be accused of inhumanity. I shall be compared to the Duke of Alba, but my duty is to obey orders, and for that reason I am here.

FIRST NOTABLE: But where will we get this amount?

MANTEUFFEL: Ah! that is *your* business.

FIRST NOTABLE: We have given our last florin.

MANTEUFFEL: Then what do you fear?

FIRST NOTABLE: What will happen, if by to-morrow this money is not paid? You would not—

MANTEUFFEL: I read the word on your lips.

Alas! yes.   I must give up the city to be pillaged.

FIRST NOTABLE: Very well; go on to the end! Take example by Nero, and set fire to the four corners of Frankfort!

MANTEUFFEL: After the pillage, perhaps.   Rome rose from her ashes more beautiful than ever. But, enough talk!   Prussia has not sent me to add one more tongue to your Republic of gabblers, her most bitter enemies.   She offers you the union of all Germany, and you ought to be thankful that it costs you so little.

THE BURGOMASTER: And suppose we could scrape together this amount, would there be any certainty of its being the last requisition?  .

MANTEUFFEL: As far as I am concerned, yes.   I pledge you my word of honour.   But I cannot vouch for a successor who may come in my place, with orders of which I know nothing. But meine Herren, I advise you, in your own interests, to pay the amount as quickly as possible; for, I tell you this in confidence, there are no severe measures they may not take against you.   They will commence to-morrow —if you do not pay—by closing the post and telegraph offices, the inns, and all the public buildings, even the breweries ; they will forbid the entry into the city of travellers and merchandise ; and that will only be the *beginning!* Now, meine Herren ! (*The* BURGOMASTER *and* NOTABLES *exeunt in consternation.*) Ah ! we will tame these proud Frankfort Republicans ! (*He looks around at the portraits of the Emperors in the Hall.*) Well ! ye old imperial majesties, are you pleased with the doings of the Prussian sword ?

## FIFTH TABLEAU.

### SCENE XII.

*Before the Royal Palace, in Berlin.*

JOHANN : Hurrah for the King ! Hurrah for Germany ! Victory !

THE CROWD : Hurrah ! Hurrah for the Queen !

WALTER (*coming out of the courtyard, on horseback*) : Meine Herren, H.M. the Queen has charged me with assuring you of the confirmation of the general reports, and which I had the honour to bring from head-quarters. Our gallant army has gained a decisive victory at Sadowa, and the war with Austria is at an end.

A Voice: Hurrah for Germany! hurrah for peace!

Walter (*answering different questions*): Yes, Colonel Herman was killed at Trentenau. (*To another*): All the first battalion of the 52nd was destroyed. (*To another*): The 2nd Landwehr had about two hundred killed, and five hundred wounded. (*Several shrieks are heard from among the crowd.*) Ah! you can't make an omelet without breaking *some* eggs.

Johann: I am a proof of that! But German patriotism is beyond proof. Hurrah for the King! Hurrah for—!

A Woman (*interrupting him*): You had better stop your noise, and go and console your worthy aunt, Frau Firzen, who is crying her heart out over the body of her only son, killed in this war, which seems to inspire you with such enthusiasm.

Johann: My poor aunt!

A Voice (*ironically*): Bah! did you not hear Captain Walter? we can't make an omelet without breaking eggs. That is all the more touching, coming from him, as one of his brothers was left at Sadowa. What! you don't shout any more, Johann!

A WOMAN (*furiously shaking her fist at the palace*) : They have killed my only son, the villains ! Who will support me now ? Who will earn bread for the other children ?

A PATRIOT : Your country will not abandon you, my good woman.

THE WOMAN : My country ! That is a word known to the poor, more by the sacrifices it exacts from them than by any good it does them. It will not be my country that will keep us from starving.

ANOTHER WOMAN : My husband is dead. All is lost for me. Ah ! I should like to catch hold of these great war-makers for one moment. Who dares to shout, Hurrah for the King ? I say that those who cause the poor to be slaughtered in this way, without reason, are miserable, cowardly brutes, and that we are great fools to allow it !

AN OLD MAN : True, true, my poor girl. But it is not after such a victory as this that the populace will listen to reason. Victory inebriates a people more than wine does an individual. Even my reason and my white hairs hardly keep me from the general intoxication. Much blood must still be shed before the vanity of princes and national prejudices give way to true wisdom and a just regard for those who have sons, brothers, fathers, or husbands to lose in this sanguinary game of war.

*Shouts and hurrahs for the* KING, BISMARCK, *and " united Germany."*

### SIXTH TABLEAU.

### SCENE XIII.

*Interior of the* WALTERS' *house.* FRAU WALTER *and* PETRUS WALTER.

FRAU WALTER (*embracing her son, and weeping*) : My boy !

PETRUS : Mother ! Having fulfilled my mission to the Queen, I hurried to find you.

FRAU WALTER : You will find all the family in mourning and tears because of Joseph's death.

PETRUS : You may, however, be proud of him, mother. He died like a hero; at the head of his company, and so covered with wounds that he was almost unrecognizable.

FRAU WALTER : I should prefer not to have him a hero, and to have him alive. Ah ! my son, if you knew what care, what anxiety, what tears are spent on a child—what, in dying, he takes from his mother's heart—you would see, even in the most glorious deaths, fewer reasons for pride than for sadness. Your brother Max is ruined, and he cannot return to Vienna. Perhaps this war has brought glory and honour to the King and his ministers; but it is certain that to many of his faithful subjects it has brought nothing but sorrow and misery. Germany may have increased; but the happiness of the German people has diminished.

PETRUS : You have too good cause for your grief, mother, that I should attempt to answer you.

FRAU WALTER : Do you think, Petrus, this dreadful war is ended ?

PETRUS : Why not ? All the Austrian forces in Germany are disorganized ; the others are kept down by our Italian allies. Besides, I have a conclusive proof, in that I am appointed military attaché to the German legation in Paris.

FRAU WALTER : My son, you make me shudder ! One evening you disappear suddenly. Two months later we learn that you have been sent to Copenhagen. At that time war breaks out with Denmark, and poor Joseph's future is spoiled. Two years later, Count von Bismarck

sends you to Gastein, Vienna, Munich, Frankfort—where else I know not—and war is immediately declared against Austria, Bavaria,
and other German States. Now you are sent
to Paris. Are we going to fight with France—
that nation, gay and frivolous if you will, but
noble and generous, among whom your sister
has found a worthy husband and many kind
friends, and from which you yourself have
chosen your future wife?

PETRUS: I know not what the future may have
in store for us, mother, but for the present
your fears are groundless. I admit that
French arrogance has more than once wounded
German pride, and that it would take but
little to turn a little diplomatic fencing into a
serious fight. But, allowing all that, national
quarrels cannot prevent esteem and affection
between individuals. For my brother-in-law,
Didier, I have an ardent attachment, and for
Louise de Montalban, a love that can never die.

FRAU WALTER: As you are going to France, I
hope that the influence of your sister and her
charming friend may change your opinion of
the wicked hatred and prejudices, which are
only too current here. Go, my boy; thought

and experience will teach you, as they have taught me, that between states and individuals it is the same thing. The happiest are those who mind their own business and are the least heard of.

# ACT III.

## DRAMATIS PERSONÆ.

KING WILLIAM I.

HIS CHIEF OF STAFF.

COUNT VON BISMARCK.

PRINCE LEOPOLD VON HOHENZOLLERN.

ABEKEN, *Friend and Counsellor.*

TRÜBE, *Chief of Police.*

AN ENVOY FROM PRINCE GORTSCHAKOFF.

GENERAL HERZOG.

COLONEL PETRUS WALTER.

BARON DE MONTALBAN.

DIDIER, *French Humanitarian.*

HERZ, } *Prussian Socialists.*
ARNOLD, }

PHILIP, *Prussian Patriot.*

LOUISE DE MONTALBAN.

WILHELMINE DIDIER.

FLORA.

## FIRST TABLEAU.

*Prelude of the Franco-German War.*

### SCENE I.

*The International Exhibition of Paris, 1867. One of the gardens of the Exhibition.*

HERZOG, WALTER, FLORA, FLITZ, *and others.* FLORA *passes, dressed rather conspicuously.*

HERZOG (*to* WALTER) : What dresses ! what manners ! Corrupt nation ! Do we ever see such things in Germany ?

FLITZ (*who has overheard*) : You refer to that lady, do you not, sir ?

HERZOG : Yes.

FLITZ : Well, she is German.

HERZOG : What inveterate jokers these Frenchmen are. You say, monsieur—

FLITZ : I say that that lady is German. As for me, I am an American.    (*Bows and exit.*)

WALTER : It is true, General. That lady with the conspicuous costume is none other than the Baroness Vinzenau, at whose house Count von Bismarck spent last evening. As for the gentleman who just spoke to us, I think I

recognize him as an American who was in
Berlin the year of the war with Denmark.

HERZOG: So there are none but strangers here?

WALTER: Oh! there are a few French people,
but so very few. Here come my sister and
her husband, and the lovely girl whose hand I
have asked in marriage.

(*Presentations and salutations.*)

## SCENE II.

HERZOG, WALTER, M. *and* MME. DIDIER, M. *and*
MDLLE. DE MONTALBAN.

WALTER: Ladies, M. le Baron, and you, my dear
Didier, allow me to present my friend, General
Herzog von der Kreussen.

(*Salutations exchanged.*)

'DIDIER: Welcome, General. France is very
proud in having so many illustrious persons
present at her grand festival of peace. Outsiders are prejudiced against us, General. Let
us hope that the gathering together of the
people at this Exhibition may serve to dissipate
some of these prejudices. France wishes to
add to her ancient glories that of having
opened the era of universal peace, and the

fraternity of nations. (*Growing animated.*) We are at the head of the conspiracy to make all men brothers; to establish an international harmony of interests, sentiments, and ideas. The old world knew only one way of making a union—by conquest. We have, as aids, printing, steam, and electricity, to help us in accomplishing the desired fusion. The state frontiers, so cut up by railways and electric telegraphs, are bound to disappear. Already war is dying out, strangled by the ever-contracting network of trade and international interests. We have laughed at the dream of the Abbot of St. Peter's. The moment is at hand when we shall hail him as the prophet of the future.

HERZOG: What did he predict?

DIDIER: The universal fraternity of nations.

HERZOG: Well—he was a fool!

DIDIER: You are wrong, General. The future will show. At any rate France will set a good example. She does not seek to contend with her neighbours, except on the ground of science, art, and industry. Those will be our future wars! That is the reason of this Exhibition, where we are happy to see you.

HERZOG : It is truly magnificent, monsieur ; but I will tell you frankly, I see nothing so remarkable as our Krupp guns.

(MONTALBAN *and* DIDIER *look at each other astounded.* HERZOG, *not noticing their astonishment, joins* WALTER *and the* LADIES.)

DIDIER (*to* MONTALBAN) : If I speak another word to that lout, I . . . I will be willing to look like him !

MONTALBAN : You are astonished, M. Didier ! But it seems to me you were one of the credulous lot who, smitten by the lovely dream of universal brotherhood, went to Berlin with the brave, long-haired Garnier-Pagès, to fraternize with the German democrats ?

DIDIER : Quite true, baron.

MONTALBAN : And the actual contact with men and things across the Rhine did not open your eyes ? You imagined in good faith that the era of national hatred was for ever past, and that if a military organization, arms and soldiers, did exist, it was only for defensive purposes. You and your friends have founded an International League of Peace. Did not your trip to Prussia convince you that you were the victims of an illusion, and of an illusion that may prove fatal ? While we are irrevocably launched in the arts of peace, Prussians and Germans think and dream of nothing but war and conquests. While we are thinking only of disarming, there the only point on which liberals and conservatives agree, is a continuous, colossal, thorough arming and equipping. The few democrats who protest against this general tendency, are suspected or qualified as traitors. In any case they wield no influence. Hatred—a fierce hatred for France—is the foundation of Prussian patriotism. These are surely the short-eared Teutomaniacs of whom Heinrich Heine speaks. As if to defy us, their chief contributions to this Exhibition are instruments of war, and such brutes as this (*pointing to* HERZOG). Think how full of brutalities must be a war, with such men for leaders !

DIDIER : All this is true, baron, but only for the Prussian Government and the Prussian nobility. The German democracy has other sentiments ; and if the Governments were to fall out, we think that its efforts, joined to those of the French democrats, would prevent a renewal of the dreadful wars of days gone by.

MONTALBAN : Another illusion, which the future will dispel, my dear Didier.　　(*Exeunt.*)

*Enter* LOUISE, WILHELMINE, WALTER, *and* HERZOG.

LOUISE (*to* WALTER) : Colonel, were you not at the Tuileries banquet yesterday ?

WALTER : Yes, mademoiselle, I was there ; but to tell you the truth, I only noticed one thing —that you were *not* there.

LOUISE : You are very gallant, Colonel; I suppose, however, that did not prevent you from seeing and hearing.　Tell me about it.

WALTER : Well, the affair went off with the utmost good feeling and courtesy on both sides.　The Emperor and Empress were charming to their guests, who will carry away with them most delightful reminiscences of their reception, as well as of this Exhibition.

LOUISE : This is very vague.　Did not some of the high officials there exchange words and sentiments—words and sentiments amicable, exalted, and which appeal to the people of the world, inviting them to study the noble emulations of peace ?

HERZOG : What struck me most was this : While the Emperor listened with a certain satisfaction to the unlimited compliments addressed to him on the subject of the Exhibition, his Majesty our most gracious King suddenly said, " But, sire, there are other things in the world besides art, commerce, and industry." "What?" asked the Emperor.  " War," answered his Majesty.

LOUISE: Ah! your gracious King said that to the Emperor! What did the Emperor reply ?

HERZOG : All who heard it, fair lady, can bear witness that he was rather abashed.  " Of course," he said, visibly embarrassed, " we must not neglect our military duties."

WALTER : The General forgets the end.  The Count von Bismarck intervened, saying, " Is war possible in such an era of civilization as ours ?  As for us, I told Colonel Stoffel lately, in Berlin, war between France and Prussia is a chimera.  You would have to come and shoot us on our own hearths, to make such a thing possible."

HERZOG : Yes, the Count said that—but—

WALTER (interrupting) : This evidently proves in error those who would ascribe to Prussia any other than the most amicable relations with all the states in general, and with France in particular.

LOUISE: Certainly, most meritorious Colonel, when we notice all the care she gives to her army, and the superb specimens of cannons on exhibition here.

WILHELMINE: Goodness! if we could only hear about something else except cannons and war! Let us go and see the flowers!

(LOUISE *and* WILHELMINE *enter a conservatory.* HERZOG *follows them.* WALTER *joins* MONTAL-BAN.)

WALTER: Baron, may I be allowed to ask for a decided answer to the proposal I have had the honour to make to you?

MONTALBAN: I wanted to delay this answer, Colonel; but as you insist, I will tell you frankly that I cannot yet decide to part with my daughter.

WALTER: May I ask the reason for this never-ending delay?

MONTALBAN: Certainly, I will tell you. I defer giving my consent simply because, notwith-standing appearances, our relations with Prussia are not of the most amicable nature, and are daily becoming less so; and I do not wish to see my son in one army and my son-in-law in another.

WALTER: What leads you to foresee such a misfortune ?

MONTALBAN: Many things. We are perhaps rather susceptible, but you are perhaps too overbearing. I do not know whether your Comte de Bismarck is conscious of what he does, but all his actions, all his words, sound to our ears like provocations. After having, up to last year, caused our Emperor to hope for territorial compensation for the aggrandizement of Prussia in Germany, in what haughty fashion were the modest demands of France repulsed, when, after the Manteuffel mission, he was confident of the support of Russia ? In the Luxemburg affair he has treated us with a stiffness and haughtiness which may be readily construed into a determination to push us to the wall. I acknowledge we are conceited; but you are in a fair way to become much more so. Prussia is more intoxicated from the smoke of Sadowa than France from all her past victories. With us, at least, lightness of character, forgetfulness of injuries, and chivalrous tendencies, compensate for the defects of national pride. The frontier of the Rhine has often been talked of and sung about, but no one ever thinks of it seriously. What is more, we are overwhelmed with humanitarian ideas of peace, which allow no time for conquests. With you it is the opposite. You remember the wars of Napoleon, and even those of Louis XIV., as if they had occurred yesterday, and you hope to be revenged when we give ourselves up to the utopia of a general disarming. Our statesmen are credulous and improvident; you, on the contrary, are all defiance, and are preparing yourselves as if the decisive struggle were to take place to-morrow. We have convened the world to a festival of peace, by this grandest and most magnificent of all universal Exhibitions; more than all else, you bring guns and cannons, and with them you prove that you hold the art of war far above all your industries. These are a few of my reasons; the others—well, I cannot tell them.

WALTER: They are most serious reasons! Perhaps you are right. In every German there are two opposite natures: that of humanity, which tells us that war is a curse; and that of our German education, which demonstrates how necessary and inevitable is a war with France. What can you expect? Since the wars of Napoleon, or even before, we have been brought up with the idea that the humiliation, the annihilation of France, is a claim upon our honour and security. Is it spite, jealousy; or simply instinct, and knowledge of danger? A little of each, probably. It is a fatal condition of affairs, in which we can do nothing, and which will not grow better, except with time. It seems to me that instead of being a reason for refusing me your daughter's hand, the situation should make your acquiescence sure. As politics are so entirely alien to questions of sentiment, it is certain that a multiplicity of marriages between nations is the best way to reunite them amicably, and to dissipate any ill-feeling and prejudice which may exist.

MONTALBAN : In a general way, this may be so; but in the present condition of affairs, your marriage would hardly prevent the impending crash between our two countries. That is why I think it prudent for my daughter's happiness still to defer this proposed union. Accept my sincere regrets, Colonel, but my resolution is taken.                    (*Bows and exit.*)

*Enter* HERZOG.

WALTER : General, Baron de Montalban, has just refused me his daughter's hand.

HERZOG : Do you love this little Frenchwoman much, Colonel ?

WALTER : Madly, General !

HERZOG : Well, when we take Paris—and that time is not far off—you will be able to take possession of her, and carry her off to Germany without asking any one's consent.

## SECOND TABLEAU.

### SCENE III.

*The King's Study in the Palace at Berlin—June,* 1870.

*The* KING *and* MEMBERS OF HIS MILITARY STAFF.

(*Maps of France and Germany spread out upon the table.*)

THE CHIEF OF THE KING'S MILITARY HOUSEHOLD (*spreading out a chart*) : Here, sire, is the map you asked for.   Say the word, and let us realize the admirable plan of campaign laid out almost two years since by the Field-Marshal, and the German army begins its victorious march to Paris.

THE KING : I share in the patriotic ardour of my people and my gallant army, general, and I am less doubtful of victory than any one. But a war with France is a serious undertaking, and we should assume too great a responsibility did we act before being sure of our power, not only from a military, but also from a diplomatic point of view. Please tell the Count von Bismarck I wish to speak with him.

(*Exeunt* OFFICERS, *leaving the* KING *studying the maps.*)

## SCENE IV.

### *The* KING, BISMARCK.

BISMARCK (*his face brightening upon seeing the King's interest in the charts*) : Has your Majesty decided to make war upon France ?

THE KING : That is just what I wished to see you about, Herr Graf.

BISMARCK : The situation can be told in two words, sire. The French are incorrigible.

You remember what occurred in August, 1866.
They had the audacity to ask for the Rhine
as far as Mayence.   I offered them—Belgium and Luxemburg.   At the same time we
sent Manteuffel to St. Petersburg.   When
they decided to accept Belgium and Luxemburg—well—Manteuffel was back again, and
we could count upon Russia.   Then I stopped
all negotiations.   Benedetti had asked for an
interview; I went off to Varzin, without waiting for him.   The following year came the
Luxemburg affair.   If Russia had not hesitated,
the result would have been entirely different
I revenged myself in the publication of the
treaties made with the south—a publication
made the very day after Rouher had from
the rostrum given his theory of *"the three
fragments."*   Well, all these petty humiliations
have not cured our old *Erbfeind*, without
deciding him to quarrel with us.   He still
imagines himself the military power of Europe.

THE KING: My brave army is eager to prove the
contrary.   Austria and the Duchies have
already felt the value of a Prussian soldier, the
soldier that I have perfected in three years.
This soldier will conquer the world; he is of

my making, he is my glory. He will only be appreciated when we have conquered France; with him we shall wipe out the disaster of Jena, and the flight at Memel.

BISMARCK: The results of the plebiscitum confirm our information in regard to the French troops actually under arms. They number hardly 350,000 men, and we can bring into the field at once twice that number. Our breech-loading cannons will cause the same disagreeable surprise to the French as our needle-guns did to the Austrians. Never was there a more favourable opportunity; never have we been stronger, and our enemy weaker, and, owing to the Mexican expedition, more thoroughly disorganized. I have a number of reports at hand, which go to prove the military disorder of France. Only yesterday Colonel Walter sent me some valuable information. What is more, in the very midst of our enemies we have a most excellent ally.

THE KING: Who?

BISMARCK (*unfolding a newspaper*): This.

THE KING: What is that?

BISMARCK: It is Rochefort's *Marseillaise;* the most widely read paper to day in Paris. It publishes every day, under the heading of "Military Tribunal," direct appeals to revolt.

THE KING: And Napoleon permits it?

BISMARCK: He prides himself on his liberalism, and is in reality nothing but a dreamer. Here is another newspaper, which tells a story of the "Pleasures of the Sword," and so contributes to the unpopularity and demoralization of the army.

THE KING: Do you pay for the publication of these articles, Herr Graf?

BISMARCK: Oh! no, sire. Providence has allowed us to economize in this respect. The French ideologists work unconsciously in the interests of the King of Prussia, so their labour is worth all the more; their praises following Düppel and Sadowa did not cost us a thaler. Between the ideologists and ourselves, France must be crushed as in a vice; but we must not allow our enemy time to look about him. Besides— and this is the decisive argument to which I would call your Majesty's attention—our situation in the interior grows each day more alarming. The southern states are strengthening their hostile attitude. I dread a union between Bavaria and Wurtemberg. The Hanoverians and Hessians—to say nothing of the little republicans of Frankfort—do not hide their complaints. The particularists every-where have carried the elections, and the most grave feature is, that all their candidates headed their programmes with " A diminution of mili-tary taxes." The deficit in the budget, result-ing from the army expenditures, has increased sensibly. Our enemy ridiculed our cannons at the Exhibition, saying, " What money thrown away ! " They would be right, were we not to use them. At any price we must get out of this absurd and dangerous situation. Besides, everything conspires to insure our success. The example of Italy ; the imprudent isolation of France ; the defiance of England, more than ever made alive to her own interests by the late lamented Prince Consort; the just resent-ment of Russia—all these, combined, have created a situation such as never occurs twice in the history of a nation. It would be a crime for a statesman not to profit by it. The pear is ripe; it must be picked. With Cato, I say, *Delenda Carthago !*

THE KING : But, Herr Graf, we cannot declare war without a motive.

BISMARCK : We declare war !　Ah, sire !　I should
be unworthy of being your Prime Minister,
did I give you such advice.　Napoleon himself
must declare war.

THE KING : How ?

BISMARCK : Listen !　The Throne of Spain is vacant.
Prim dare not occupy it.　I had thought of
offering it to the Duc de Montpensier, but
since his duel with the Infant Henri that is
impossible.　Why should we not place at
Madrid a member of the great house of
Hohenzollern ?

THE KING : There is already one at Bucharest,
who would only be too glad to leave.

BISMARCK : Never mind.　We cannot accustom
the people of Europe too much to Prussian
princes.　Besides, it is not so much a matter
of placing a Hohenzollern at Madrid, as of
offering an insult to the French which may
make them lose the little head they have left.
To make the pill more bitter, we can remind
Napoleon of how kindly he received Prince Leopold and his sister at the Tuileries, in 1867.　It
will then be simply an agreeable surprise that we
wished to give him—like that of Prince Charles
of Roumania, who was also well patronized.

THE KING : Well; send for Prince Leopold.

BISMARCK : I have already done so, sire ; he is here.

## SCENE V.

*The* KING, BISMARCK, LEOPOLD VON HOHENZOLLERN.

THE KING : Prince, I have good news for you. We have resolved to make you King of Spain.

LEOPOLD : Sire, will you kindly allow me to decline the honour ?

THE KING (*sternly*) : The princes of the royal family of Prussia must obey without reasoning. I have told you my wishes. Herr Graf, you will write to General Prim that Prince Leopold von Hohenzollern accepts the crown of Spain, and that the King of Prussia, as head of the house of Hohenzollern, makes no opposition.

(*Exit* LEOPOLD, *then the* KING.)

## SCENE VI.

BISMARCK *alone.*

BISMARCK (*writing to Field-Marshal Von Moltke*) : " Herr Graf, I have decided the King to allow Prince Leopold von Hohenzollern to accept the throne of Spain. In three weeks or a

month the German army must be ready to
enter France." (*To an officer*): Have this
letter given at once to Field-Marshal Von
Moltke. (*Looking at his watch*): Now, I can
be off to Varzin. I have not lost my day.

## THIRD TABLEAU.

### Scene VII.

*A Cabinet-maker's Workshop.*

Arnold (Foreman), Herz, Philip, *and* other
Workmen.

Arnold: You seem very gay, Philip!

Philip: I have just heard some news.

Omnes: What?

Philip: Prince Leopold von Hohenzollern is
named King of Spain.

Arnold: Prince Leopold! But he has never
been there; does he even know how to speak
Spanish?

Philip: What does that matter! The King and
Count von Bismarck have appointed him; the
Spaniards have only to accept him.

A Workman: I would not have thought, comrade, that Prince Leopold's success could have made you so gay.

PHILIP: You don't understand that it means war with France.

ARNOLD: The devil it does! Why?

PHILIP: Do you imagine that French pride and vanity will support quietly the coronation of a Prussian prince at Madrid?

ARNOLD: So then *we* are seeking the quarrel—a genuine German quarrel! (*Some of the Workmen laugh.*) My young friends, you do wrong to rejoice at the prospect of a conflict the result of which can only be the death and mutilation of thousands of honest people, and —who knows?—perhaps the invasion of our own country; not to speak of the serious injury it must do to labour—to workmen as well as employers.

PHILIP: You are right, it will be hard; but we shall conquer, and then we can make the enemy pay the expenses of the war. For some time General von Moltke has been preparing, and we are sure of our victory.

ARNOLD: Then it is not war, but a slaughter.

PHILIP: War is seldom anything else. Do you love the French? Do you not know, that so long as they exist there can be no peace for Europe ? It will be a glorious thing for Germany to bring them to reason.

ARNOLD : Evidently we do not understand words and their meaning in the same way. You others, who are young, call Glory what is often nothing but the bloody reflex of a human massacre. I only admit true glory to be that founded upon justice, or upon valuable services rendered to one's country or to humanity. I cannot reconcile myself to this shedding of blood, except in case of a legitimate defense; and I have no faith in these quarrels, in which honour—too often a myth—is but a plaything. We have fought already with Denmark and Austria, and we have won. Our national pride is exalted ; but I think, that in the Divine scale, where all is weighed impartially, the side of glory and conquests will be the less heavy of the two. What mountains of mangled corpses, what ruins, have invariably been the consequence of these enterprises. Three of our workmen left their bones to whiten at Sadowa, as you perhaps, Philip, will leave yours in France. Having brought Austria and Denmark to reason, we must now do the same thing with France; for it seems there is no one reasonable in all Europe, but ourselves. Do they think there are not enough widows and orphans in Germany? Ah, my poor Philip! can you not see that in such cases the people are always the dupes, and that whatever tends to cause human beings to murder each other, is neither glorious nor profitable, but only merits the contempt of sensible men?

PHILIP: It is useless to reason with you, Arnold. Politics have nothing to do with morality. The end justifies the means. It is for the establishment of a lasting peace that we wish to crush France.

ARNOLD: The French said nothing but that, when, at the commencement of this century, they oppressed us with a most unbearable yoke.

PHILIP: You argue well, Arnold, but your words are not in season; and as our work is over, you will allow us to drink at the neighbouring brewery to the defeat of the French, and the coming victory of the German arms.

(*The* WORKMEN *leave.*)

HERZ: Friend Arnold, you waste your breath. In the actual condition of affairs, they will

*not* listen to reason.  This policy of blood and
iron, which you so rightly stigmatize, will
bring nearer the hour when Germany must
learn to see, hear, think, and act by herself.
Influenced by dynastic and personal prejudices,
rather than by the honour and interests of the
country, the King and his cabinet to-day cause
a quarrel between two nations, who never
asked for anything but to live in peace ; an
unholy war, in which the victors will be the
vanquished, for victory will only madden them,
whereas defeat will inspire the vanquished with
many useful reflections.  Notwithstanding all
his foresight, Bismarck does not realize, that,
in rousing Germany from her long slumber,
he has awakened a lioness who will sleep no
·more, and who will ask and require from her
keepers other things, and more, than have heretofore been given.  Ah, my noble Count ! you
can conquer Europe, but in so doing you
render more assured the triumph of democracy,
the people's cause.  Thanks to you, the red
flower of German progress will bloom ten or
twenty years sooner.  O conceited King !
you are mistaken if you fancy that you can
monopolize for yourself and nobles all the

fruits of victory. If you do not compensate the people and their liberties, as you shower gifts upon your generals—well, we will see, after the war !

## FOURTH TABLEAU.

*The scene is laid at Ems, July 13th, 1870.*

### SCENE VIII.

BISMARCK, TRÜBE, *and* ABEKEN.

BISMARCK (*just arrived from Varzin, to his* SECRETARY) : Are Trübe and Abeken arrived ?

THE SECRETARY : Yes, your Excellency, here they are. (*Exit.*)

BISMARCK (*to* TRUBE): Tell me what has been going on since you sent your last report ; and be precise in regard to the action and attitude of the French Ambassador.

TRÜBE : Herr Graf, the French Ambassador arrived here the 8th. He had an interview with his Majesty the day following. The King answered by a very polite but decided refusal, saying that he only knew of the affair as head of the family, not as King of Prussia ;

and further, that he dare not interfere, and run the risk of wounding the feelings of the Spaniards.

BISMARCK : Well ?

TRÜBE : M. Benedetti saw his Majesty again on the 10th. The King said he had received no answer from Prince Leopold. The Ambassador came again on the 11th, but without success, his Majesty always refusing to interfere. Yesterday, another interview, another question, another refusal. His Majesty did not speak of Prince Leopold's renunciation, although he had been informed of it.

BISMARCK : And to-day ?

TRÜBE : The Ambassador waited upon the King this morning, and broached the subject of Prince Leopold's renunciation, asking his Majesty to prevent, if necessary, a renewal of the prince's candidacy. His Majesty refused.

BISMARCK (*to* ABEKEN): What is the last news from France ?

ABEKEN : Capital for us, Herr Graf. The Lord of Paris is furious, and construes the Hohenzollern matter into a personal insult. The parliamentary opposition is on the alert, ready to accuse him of folly and temerity if he raises the gauntlet, and of cowardice if he bears the affront.

BISMARCK: That is as it should be. France would not make me lie. *She* shall declare war. (*To* TRÜBE): But I told you to look after Leopold; why did you allow him to renounce the throne of Spain?

TRÜBE: My agent followed him like his shadow. It was not Prince Leopold, but his father, who signed the renunciation.

BISMARCK: Happily I could follow this intrigue from Varzin, and I have made it serve our own purposes. Our agents in Paris have used it to make Napoleon exact new demands from us. Not only must he be in the wrong, but the wrong must be a flagrant one, so as to insure us the neutrality of Europe, which, all the same, would be powerless against the strength of United Germany. Here is what happens: Napoleon asks from the royal hand, written promises for the future. His ambassador has dared inflict this humiliation upon our august sovereign.

ABEKEN: The occurrence took place as you say, but in a most inoffensive way. Everything passed off most courteously. To tell the truth, his Majesty was embarrassed; he was waiting for you, Herr Graf.

BISMARCK: Well, here I am (*after a few moments' writing*). Here is the despatch, which you must send through the Wolff Agency to all the newspapers of Europe. Read it!

TRÜBE (*reads*): "After the news of Prince Leopold's renouncement had been communicated to the French Government, the French ambassador at Ems asked in addition, from his Majesty the King, a promise that in all future time he would refuse his consent should the house of Hohenzollern renew the application of their candidate. The King thereupon, through his aide-de-camp, notified the ambassador of France that, having nothing more to communicate upon this subject, he must refuse any further interviews."

ABEKEN: But this is not true, Herr Graf! The truth is—

BISMARCK: —In the mistake. If his Majesty did not send this message in these words, it is only because politeness forbade it. But as we are dealing in politics and not in politeness— (*enter a* SECRETARY)—What is it?

THE SECRETARY: The messenger from Prince

Gortschakoff, for whom your Excellency was waiting.

BISMARCK : Show him in. (*To* TRÜBE *and* ABEKEN: Return, when this messenger has gone. I will keep this despatch yet a while.

## SCENE IX.

### BISMARCK *and a* RUSSIAN DIPLOMAT.

BISMARCK: Monsieur, the decisive moment has arrived. France threatens us. Her vanity urges her on to her own destruction. The fate of arms must decide between us. The Czar Nicholas will be avenged. Each nation of the south and west has had its day, it is now the turn of Russia and Prussia. That is the substance of what I said to the prince-chancellor. He said you would bring me the answer.

THE RUSSIAN : The prince answers, Herr Graf, that he loves France no more than you; but he thinks you are starting too great an enterprise, with incalculable consequences. If you are beaten, France comes out of the fight immeasurably bettered, and who knows what influence her victory might have in Poland?

If you win, new and serious questions arise. Old Europe is such a tumble-down edifice, that you can hardly touch one stone without endangering the safety of the whole.

BISMARCK : We should rebuild it anew.

THE RUSSIAN : On what basis ?

BISMARCK : We guarantee to Russia entire liberty of action in the east; let Russia guarantee us the same liberty in the west.

THE RUSSIAN : The prince-chancellor accepts this compact, and makes a note of your promise. If you feel strong, begin your march at once. The souvenirs of the Crimea, the French policy during the Polish insurrection, the friendship existing between our two sovereigns, —all these can assure you of Russia's watchful but sympathetic neutrality.

*(Bows and exit.)*

## SCENE X.

BISMARCK, *then* TRÜBE *and* ABEKEN, *followed by* VON MOLTKE.

BISMARCK : Truly, were I not alive I should say that there is nothing so stupidly blind as a diplomat ! Gortschakoff is no more far-seeing than the rest of them. In allowing us to whip France, he is doubly of service to our policy : for once having beaten the *Erbfeind* of the west, by the same blow we have outwitted the *Erbfeind* of the east, in depriving him of his only possible ally. Gortschakoff has the same ideas as Napoleon had in 1866. He imagines that the struggle will be long, and that both Germany and France will come out of the contest much weakened. The near future will show him his error. In truth, the surest policy, is to know how to profit by others' mistakes. (*Enter* TRÜBE *and* ABEKEN.) Meine Herren, have this despatch forwarded at once to the Wolff Agency. (*Exeunt* TRÜBE *and* ABEKEN.) Now we shall see how France can get out of this (*rings*). Has Field-Marshal Von Moltke arrived ?

A SECRETARY : He has just come.

*Enter* MOLTKE.

BISMARCK ı Herr Graf, the time has come for me to give you the order of mobilization, signed by his Majesty before my departure for Varzin. Here it is. You can put in the date of the declaration of war, when those Parisian idiots send it. (*Exit* BISMARCK.)

K

MOLTKE: At last! The time has come. Ah! France will have to pay dearly for the First Napoleon's victories, and the improvidence of Napoleon III. (*To some members of his staff*): Gentlemen, we shall be in Paris in a month!

# ACT IV.

## Dramatis Personæ.

King William I.
Count von Bismarck.
Field-Marshall von Moltke.
General Herzog.
Russian Military Attaché.
Austrian Military Attaché.
Italian Military Attaché.
Busch, *Bismarck's Secretary.*
Trübe, *Chief of Police.*
Lobemberg, *Jewish Banker.*
Schwartz, *Lieutenant of Artillery.*
Richard Wagner, *the Composer.*
Hidalgo, *Spanish Diplomat.*
Flitz.
Aristides, *his Servant.*
Baron de Montalban.
Louise, *his Daughter.*
Rollin, *Captain in the French Army.*
Another Captain in the French Army.
An Æronaut.
A wounded French Soldier.

A WOUNDED SAXON SOLDIER.
THE GHOST OF CHARLEMAGNE.
THE GHOST OF NAPOLEON I.
JOHNSON,
JEAN DURAND, } *in the Audience.*

## FIRST TABLEAU.

### The Battle of Sedan.

#### SCENE I.

*A height overlooking the field of Sedan. Time,
Sept. 1st, 1870.*

HERZOG, FLITZ, OFFICERS *and* SOLDIERS.

HERZOG : What is the name of that village where
the inhabitants fired upon the Bavarians ?

AN OFFICER : Bazeilles.

HERZOG : Go and tell the Bavarian commander to
set fire to it. It will teach these French
peasants what it costs to shoot at German
soldiers. Wherever you meet with resistance,
do not hesitate to make an example. Above
all, shoot down the priests, mayors, and magis-
trates, to punish them for not having restrained
their people. It will be doing the French a
service, as there will not be so many left to
make fools of themselves. Go ! (*The soldiers*

*exeunt.*) Good day, mein Herr, you see how we are playing with the *Great Nation.* Bazaine's army, the only one which could in any way compare with ours, is tightly blocked up in Metz by Prince Frederick Charles, and can only come out as our prisoners. Napoleon, defeated at Sedan, will soon surrender with what is left of MacMahon's army. The war is over, and we shall soon know under what conditions the peace will be signed.

FLITZ : There is, in fact, no question of your triumph, General. I hope your Government will make use of it with wisdom, or at least moderation.

(*Exit* HERZOG, *smiling significantly.*)


## SCENE II.

*The* KING *and his* STAFF, BISMARCK, FOREIGN OFFICERS, *all following with field-glasses the movements of the battle. On the right Bazeilles is seen in flames. At different points columns of smoke bear witness to the continuance of the fight.*

THE KING : Our victory is even more complete than at Sadowa. Praise be to the Almighty, whose powerful protection has made our army invincible.

BISMARCK : This is indeed an ending that Napoleon little expected, when he received us with such pomp and ostentation at his marvellous Exhibition of 1867!

AN AIDE-DE-CAMP (*coming up*) : Sire, the French propose to surrender. Field-Marshal von Moltke exacts an unconditional capitulation, and has asked the enemy to send an officer to visit our fortifications, and to satisfy himself of the impossibility of their escape. General Reille, the Emperor's aide-de-camp, will be here shortly. He is commissioned to arrange an interview between your Majesty and the Emperor.

BISMARCK : I will go to meet Napoleon III., but your Majesty cannot receive him before he has signed the capitulation of the entire French army.

(*Columns of smoke are seen rising from the town of Sedan.*)

BISMARCK : Look, sire ! the Napoleonic empire ends in smoke.

THE KING : Now, I think, our revenge for Jena is complete.

BISMARCK : You are wrong, sire. Do you forget that Napoleon I. entered Berlin? that he forced the authorities of the capital to deliver him the keys of the city on a silver dish? Do you forget the outrages heaped upon Queen Louise? Your mother dying of cold and hunger in her flight to Memel; her final torture and death by the slow pain of the Treaty of Tilsit—are these memories effaced from your heart?

THE KING : No, these are things one cannot forget.

BISMARCK : When the time comes for the peace negotiations, your Majesty will see that his faithful Minister has also not forgotten.

(*Exeunt the* KING *and his* STAFF, *and* BISMARCK.)

## SCENE III.

*The outskirts of the battle; detachments of troops pass; wounded soldiers are carried by.*

FLITZ, ARISTIDES, *and the* FOREIGN OFFICERS.

ITALIAN OFFICER : Near here a batallion of Zouaves fought desperately. But of what use are swords against cannons? Ah! my poor comrades of Palestro and Magenta!

ANOTHER OFFICER : Over there, at Bazeilles, the
Bavarians forced men, women, and children
indiscriminately into their burning homes.

*A French regiment of prisoners, with their Prus-
sian escort, pass. The Prussian band play
tauntingly the "Marseillaise," changing the
refrain, "Aux armes, citoyens!" to "Marl-
borough s'en va-t-en guerre!"*

AUSTRIAN OFFICER : France was growing tiresome
to us, with her victories and her pride. Alas!
to-day she only excites compassion.

*Enter the* RUSSIAN MILITARY ATTACHÉ.

THE RUSSIAN : Do you know the conclusion, monsieur ? Napoleon has sent his sword to King
William. I did not love France, but, believe
me, I am frightened at her downfall, and at
the space she will leave vacant in Europe.
Now that she is no longer to be dreaded, I
remember all her chivalry, and all her noble
qualifications. I remember with what courtesy
the French ended the Crimean war, to the
disgust and disappointment of our bitterest
enemy, England. I already begin to feel the
same anxiety that the French experienced
after Sadowa. Ah! I fear Russia made a

great mistake in thus allowing the annihilation of her generous adversary.

FLITZ; She will be guilty of a still greater blunder if she allows the completion of the projects of conquest proposed by the Prussian Cabinet.

## SCENE IV.

FLITZ *alone with* ARISTIDES ; *then* TRÜBE.

*The negro has lifted the dead body of a General, and placed it against a stone.*

ARISTIDES : Massa Flitz, dat dead gin'ral ain't no heavier nor a dead private.

FLITZ : *Quot libras in duce summo !* Juvenal never thought his words would be quoted by a wretched darkey.

ARISTIDES (*looking at the corpse*) : Massa, he looks as if he was 'live, and was goin' to speak !

FLITZ : Could he speak, he would probably say that all the politics of the noble conqueror and ex-noble conquered in the scales of common sense weigh less than his own mangled body.

ARISTIDES : Massa, dere's ten hundred million corpses. Golly ! I never—

FLITZ : Shut up !

> (ARISTIDES *busies himself in robbing the bodies of the dead;* FLITZ *muses.*)

FLITZ : Poor France ! unfortunate Germany ! Ah ! if only my efforts could bring about this peace from which to-day a stream of blood separates you. Hallo ! There is Bismarck, reporting to the King his interview with the setting Cæsar. The rising Cæsar is radiant. There he goes, into his tent to dream of new triumphs. What a lot of poor devils for whom all dreams are at an end ! Ah ! who is this ? Trübe ; he will answer my purpose, and help me carry out my project. (*To* TRÜBE) : Mein Herr, I wish to speak to Count von Bismarck.

TRÜBE : His Excellency is very much fatigued with the work of the day, and can receive no one before to-morrow.

FLITZ : Political matters cannot be put off till the morrow, especially under existing circumstances. I ask you formally to deliver this letter to his Excellency, and without delay.

> (TRÜBE *takes the letter, and exit.* BISMARCK *appears shortly after.*)

## Scene V.

### Bismarck *and* Flitz.

Bismarck : Is it you, mein Herr, who have sought an interview with me by sending this letter?

Flitz : Myself, Herr Graf.

Bismarck : The eminent statesman who wrote it is apparently a friend of yours; he wishes me to grant you a few moments that I may learn the opinion of free America upon the events of Europe. I am at your service.

Flitz : My task, Herr Graf, is very simple. America foresaw your victory, and will greet it with pleasure; for the Mexican expedition and the moral support given to the South have wonderfully weakened our former sympathy for France. America—not the Government itself, for that I cannot say I represent—but the American people say to you through me : As you are strong, be magnanimous !

Bismarck : We are both, mein Herr. The proof of it is that we shall only ask of France a war indemnity of eight or ten billions, and the cession of Alsace and Lorraine.

Flitz : Will you kindly tell me what you would exact did you abuse your victory ?

BISMARCK: We should ask for twenty billions, and take the French territory as far as the Loire; no one can prevent our doing so.

FLITZ: Very true; but how long would this condition of things last? You know perfectly that the result would be an eternal war in Europe; that it would excite envy and jealousy under which Germany of 1871 must succumb, notwithstanding her admirable military organization and the genius of her statesmen and generals—as France of 1815 succumbed, even with Napoleon I. at its head.

BISMARCK: On the other hand, mein Herr, you must understand that the French will never forgive us their defeat; that sooner or later a new war with them is inevitable; and that now the most ordinary prudence causes us to take needful precautions.

FLITZ: The most serious and safest precautions, Herr Graf, are the ones which I advise. The world's sympathy, which is to-day yours, would, if you abused of your victory, soon be for your enemies, whose weakness is not altogether caused by their vices. Perhaps you would not so easily have triumphed over France had she not been given up to generous illusions—had she not so innocently believed in a new era of reason and fraternity—had she not prematurely destroyed the false gods, for so long, and even yet to-day, worshipped by the rest of Europe. Forgive my American freedom of speech—but do not force the world to look upon your victory as an abuse of confidence. True victory is that which you can gain to-day, and which will win the approval of the old and new worlds. Having conquered France, learn to conquer yourselves, in repressing those ideas of vain-glory and victory which trouble the spirits of all conquerors. Impose upon France a just indemnity—but beyond that, nothing. Do not touch their territory. In this way you will acquire a glory superior to that of all your predecessors, and comparable only to that of our great Washington. France itself will admire you, and, willing or not, will find herself disarmed by your magnanimity. You will thus lay a firm foundation for the eternal peace of Germany and the world.

BISMARCK: We start, mein Herr, from such entirely different points, that I doubt if we can really understand each other. You seem to think that men were made simply to look at and

admire each other; I, basing my reasoning
upon human nature, think that they must in-
evitably quarrel, and often kill each other.
History, which is better than all your ideology,
shows us that civilization and progress can only
be gained at this price. Fire, iron, and blood
were needed to make Germany and regenerate
France. Well, there they are.

FLITZ: If history shows that this happens only
too often, conscience and religion agree in
declaring that it could and should be otherwise.
Besides, in adopting these sad facts as principles one could go to any length. We have
the same belief, Herr Graf. Christ taught love,
and forgiveness of injuries. He allowed Himself to be crucified.

BISMARCK: That is, perhaps, not the best thing
he did. In politics we must crucify our enemies, or later on they will crucify us.

FLITZ: There is, Herr Graf, another field of
battle, or, rather, of emulation, upon which
you could challenge and meet your enemies : I
mean the struggle with nature, against igno-
rance and prejudice. On this ground America
strives with the whole world. Grant peace—a
just peace—to the vanquished. Do not bleed

them by taking from them a territory which years of possession have made their own. Think of what the Venetian bullets cost the Austrians. Be a conqueror of a new sort, that will excite the admiration of the whole world. You smile, Herr Graf, but take care that France does not occupy this place which you leave vacant. Take care you do not lose your only chance of being truly great.

BISMARCK : All that is very pretty, mein Herr, but rather impracticable. Now I will speak to you frankly. Even though I should be in the humour to follow your advice, it would be impossible to persuade the King and his military household. Why ask the Prussians to be better than other men ? We are conquerors, and we profit by our conquests, as has always been done. We take back Alsace and Lorraine, which Louis XIV. stole from us two centuries ago.

FLITZ : But the people of Alsace and Lorraine don't want you !

BISMARCK : When a child has left his father's roof to dwell with mountebanks and ruffians, and, when corrupted by these, he refuses to return, it is the father's duty to use force. This is what we will do, if necessary. First, let us obtain the legitimate return for our blood shed. Magnanimity after prudence! You will excuse me, mein Herr; I think we have nothing further to say to each other. You are a great philosopher; but the world belongs to men of action. (*Bows and exit.*)

Flitz (*alone*): It is written above that success blinds the most far-seeing. Ah, human progress! you are too much like a crab! Well, courage! according to this man's ideas the massacre has only begun. (*Going to his horse*): Come here, Potomac. Thank God you are a quadruped, for never was there a quadruped such a fool as this biped with whom I have been speaking. (*Mounts his horse.*)

A Prussian Officer: Make haste, mein Herr, to join the staff. The army has received its orders to march upon Paris.

### SECOND TABLEAU.

#### *A Dream.*

#### Scene VI.

Johnson, Durand, *and the Characters of the Dream.*

Durand: The scene has changed, has it not

Johnson? I see a town, but surely it is not Sedan, for I see no heaps of bloody corpses and broken arms. What is this?

JOHNSON. Do you not recognize the dome of the Invalides? King William is asleep, and his thoughts are in Paris. He goes into the Church of the Invalides, and sets fire to all the old battle-flags and banners, the French trophies of victory. He approaches the mausoleum of Napoleon, to take his sword and crown. Napoleon rises; his lips move; the man of marble speaks. Listen!

*(The statue of* NAPOLEON I. *appears.)*

NAPOLEON: *Qui va là?*

KING WILLIAM: The revenge of Germany! The vanquished of Jena, led by one of the sons of Queen Louise, have, this time alone, invaded the French soil. On every side they have beaten Germany's ancient oppressors, and thy nephew, the Emperor of the French, has just delivered his sword to me.

NAPOLEON: I had hoped that my history would have disabused the French and Germans, and the whole world, of the smoke of false glory. If I did not bear such a responsibility for the events thou hast related, I should curse you both—thee and my nephew—for the rivers of blood you have caused to flow. When thou shalt join me, beyond the grave, blind and spiteful old man, thou shalt find how painful and dishonourable arc these laurels which now thou wearest, but which then thou shalt feel, as I do, a crown of thorns. (KING WILLIAM *seems appalled.*) Hast thou not read in my Memoirs of St. Helena, my prophecy, "In fifty years Europe will be Cossack or Republican"? Hast thou thought of the day when Russia shall rouse the Sclavonic race against Germany, even as thou hast raised the Germanic race against France? What will become of Germany, if the Sclavs bring to bear in this struggle the spite and hatred thou hast just shown toward France? All civilized Europe combined could not resist this Sclavonic wave; and now, instead of insuring to thyself the aid of France, thou hast made Russia our natural ally! Thy Prime Minister has justly ridiculed my nephew, who, in dread of Austria, has thrown himself into the merciless power of Germany. Dost thou think that the future will judge less severely those who by hatred of

France shall have thrown Germany into the formidable clasp of France and Russia?

NAPOLEON *vanishes. The scene changes to the old cathedral of Aix-la-Chapelle, with the tomb of* CHARLEMAGNE. *The old* EMPEROR *has in his hand the sphere of the world. The statue seems alive.*

CHARLEMAGNE (*withdrawing his hand from* KING WILLIAM, *who snatches at the sphere*): Thou wouldst take this sphere, poor, proud fool! Know that this power which so intoxicates thee is but an imperceptible dot in the world's great page. Look around this grand space, where thou spreadest barbarity when thou shouldst restrain it. Frederick-William! thou art even more guilty than Napoleon I., for thou hast had his faults before thee, by which to profit. I was Emperor of the Franks, that is, of the French and German. I ruled over this grand union of races formed by the Gauls, Romans, and innumerable other tribes, who from beyond the Further-Rhine came every century to join the Gallo-Roman body. The glorious Roman Empire understood all the elements of civilization of my time, and spread out to the north,

south, east, and west, repressing or subduing
the pagans and savages. All our wars were
holy and civilizing. Yours of to-day, French
and Germans, are but sacrilegious, impious
fratricides. Shame and curses upon those who
have caused the two halves of my dominion to
quarrel! Shame and curses on those who
have sown hatred in generous hearts!

(CHARLEMAGNE *disappears.*)

DURAND: Heaven and earth are wrapped in the
darkness of night. Who are these three phantoms rising from the horizon?

JOHNSON: These phantoms will, at a given moment, become terrible realities. From them
George III. learned the surrender of Corn-
wallis; Napoleon saw them at Waterloo. It
is useless to name them, as they are only
visible to the eye of the philosopher and poet,
while to conquerors they are always invisible.
Let us simply say, as to a ray of sunshine on a
gloomy day, *au revoir !*

DURAND: What does the old King say to this?

JOHNSON: He seems much moved; but to-morrow, drunk with the smoke of worldly glory,
he will have forgotten it all. So goes the

world. Great thoughts and noble sentiments
vanish like a dream. But evil rests heavily,
and incrusts itself upon the heart of man,
although its contact is anything but cheerful.

## THIRD TABLEAU.

*The Prussians at Versailles.*

### Scene VII.

Bismarck's *work-room in the Palace of Versailles.*
Bismarck, Trübe, Busch, *then* Loremberg.

Bismarck : The Minister of the King of Prussia
dictating his orders in the palace of the Great
King ! It is a pity that Louis XIV. and
Louvois are dead. I should have asked them
to dinner. (*To his* Secretary) : Busch, this
evening you will write an article for the German papers on the Treaty of 870, the one
made between Charles-the-Bald and Louis-the-
Germanic, which fixed the first German frontier, dividing Lorraine into two parts. We
must increase the capital of these reptiles. I
hate all these ink-bugs, but if we must despise
them we must also, if possible, pay them.

*Enter* TRÜBE *with several newspaper clippings.*

BISMARCK: What is this?

TRÜBE: An article by Feuerbach.

BISMARCK: What says this old professor of Halle?

TRÜBE: He condemns the German victories, cries " *Væ Victoribus,*" and says the future is for the vanquished.

BISMARCK: Is that all?

TRÜBE: He says that the smoke of glory blown away, Germany will wake to find itself in Prussian chains; that an Empire will destroy Germany, as it has destroyed France; that Alsace and Lorraine will be a Poland and Venetia for us; that the war indemnity will only be used to make new cannons, and enrich Krupp, whom he calls the purveyor of death; and that we shall be condemned to an eternal war.

BISMARCK: Have the newspapers seized which dare to publish these tirades, but do not molest the author. We must forgive these old professors, as we would a lot of old women, some liberties of speech. What is Jacoby doing?

TRÜBE: He presided again this week at a democratic meeting, where they harangued against

a continuation of the war, and the seizure of
Alsace and Lorraine.

BISMARCK: Have him arrested, and sent to the
fortress of Kœnigsberg, so that he will not
preside at any more such meetings. We will
let him out again when the peace is signed.

TRÜBE: A man carrying this letter, addressed to
his Majesty, was this morning arrested here.

BISMARCK: Let us see; (*reads*): "To William,
King of Prussia. Old man, when you appear
before your God, what good will you derive
from an addition of territory covered with
ruins, corpses, and blood? Soon a few square
feet of earth will suffice for your resting-place!
Signed, Delmas, Protestant Pastor of La
Rochelle." Just like a Frenchman. With
grand speeches they hope to cure the effects
of their folly. Let this poor man go, but have
him put out of Versailles.

TRÜBE: Herr Graf, a Nancy newspaper has pub-
lished an article in large type, as follows: "I
believe in God, I do not believe in strength.
Justice alone is stable. These events are not
results to be accepted quietly, but hard
places to be climbed, and only on condition
that each event finds us better on the morrow,

and more fully prepared. This is my political belief."

BISMARCK : I think the author has been put in prison.

TRÜBE : At first, this was done by the Prefect ; but the author having proved that it was only the reproduction of a letter of Queen Louise after Jena, they now wait your instructions.

BISMARCK : Make the punishment doubly severe, for his having dared to put the words of a Queen of Prussia in the mouth of a Frenchman.

BUSCH : Here is a despatch, Herr Graf, from his Majesty's Ambassador at St. Petersburg. I have just translated it.

BISMARCK (reads) : " From good authority I learn that last evening, at a banquet given in the . palace, the Czar proposed the health of the conqueror of Sedan ; this the Czarewitch refused to drink, and in so doing broke his glass." The Czarewitch is a little imprudent. He can break as many glasses as he wants. Now that France is beaten, we have not so much need of the Russian alliance. (Enter LOREMBERG.) What do you wish, Loremberg ?

LOREMBERG : I come, Herr Graf, to ask your powerful intervention in the French municipalities, upon which you have levied heavy contributions, and which declare themselves as unable to pay. I am ready to loan them, upon good security of course, the necessary amounts.

BISMARCK : I understand. That is a capital idea of yours, Loremberg. Here is a word to Field-Marshal von Moltke ; he himself will present you to the French mayors. You can begin with the Mayor of St. Germain-en-Laye, whose regrets I have again received to-day. Lend him what he needs, Loremberg, but squeeze 10,000 francs pin-money out of him for Countess Vinzenau. Trübe will hand it to her. By the way, Loremberg, when you see your friend Rothschild, tell him we are very much displeased at our reception by his representative at Ferrières. He deserved to have his chateau destroyed. Go !

(Exit LOREMBERG.)

*A* SERVANT *brings a tray with wine and glasses.*
TRÜBE *and* BISMARCK *drink.*

BISMARCK : What delicious wines these Frenchmen make! (*To* TRÜBE): Well! Paris has not yet surrendered?

TRÜBE: It will not hold out for long, Herr Graf. The Field-Marshal thinks it will be about Christmas. Perhaps we can find out something definite from an individual who pretends to be a Spanish diplomat, and who represented himself to the outposts as an acquaintance of yours.

BISMARCK: Show him in.

## SCENE VIII.

### *The same.* HIDALGO.

BISMARCK: Ah! it is you, M. Hidalgo. I have not had the pleasure of seeing you since you represented Spain in Germany. There are, then, some diplomats still in Paris?

HIDALGO: Probably, M. le Comte, as they wrote you only lately, asking for the free passage of their sealed despatches, which you refused.

BISMARCK: Very true. Could I have done otherwise?

HIDALGO: No one complains; so you must be right. May I ask after the health of the Comtesse de Bismarck?

BISMARCK : Oh ! she is much better, since her son is better. She has only one complaint, her hatred of the Gauls, whom she wishes to see all burnt, or exterminated by force of arms ; even the little children, who are not responsible for having such abominable parents.

HIDALGO : Oh, M. le Comte, I protest for the Comtesse, at least in what concerns the little children.

(*Bismarck offers a glass of wine to Hidalgo.*)

BISMARCK : Your good health, M. Hidalgo.

HIDALGO : Your health, M. le Comte.

BISMARCK (*straddling his chair, his face beaming*) : Are you not charged with some mission to us, M. Hidalgo ?

HIDALGO : Not the slightest.

BISMARCK : I thought perhaps— We know perfectly well that the Parisians only ask to surrender, and are only prevented by the usurpers of the Hôtel de Ville.

HIDALGO : If you said just the contrary, you would be nearer the truth. I should even be unjust to the Government of National Defence in crediting them with an intention to surrender ; although they appreciate much better than the populace the inconveniences of a prolonged resistance.

BISMARCK : At any rate we know that if they do not surrender, they will starve to death by thousands.

HIDALGO : I thought, M. le Comte, it was not allowed to contemplate such a state of affairs unfeelingly !

BISMARCK : What would you have us do ? You know the proverb :. Better kill the devil, than let him kill you. We cannot leave Paris. The Parisians are such fools, they would look upon themselves as conquerors if we did not occupy their city. Besides, the King and the army wish to enter Babylon, and they shall enter. I cannot understand the absurd obstinacy of the Parisians, in prolonging a useless resistance.

HIDALGO : They may wish to give you a better opinion of themselves.

BISMARCK : The populace has again alarmed the Government of the Hôtel de Ville ?

HIDALGO : The populace itself seems to have sworn to change your opinion, on their score. They have even raised by subscription enough to buy a cannon, which they have named, " The Populace."

BISMARCK : There is French energy for you ! But

you will acknowledge that ours is equal to it, when we take this cannon, along with the others, to Berlin before they have a chance to use it. You see, my Spanish friend, you made a mistake in not taking our Hohenzollern. The Latin race is played out. It has done great things in its day; but now its day is over, it is gradually diminishing, and soon will disappear completely. The Germanic race is, so to speak, the male principle, which traverses Europe, enriching it. The Sclavonic and Celtic races are the female principle. The former principle extends North as far as the Northern Ocean; west, to England—

BUSCH (*interrupting*) : To America.

BISMARCK : Yes, there are the children, the fruits of our race. The French were of no importance, except so long as the Germanic element, the Francs, were at the head of the nation. In the revolution of 1789 the Germanic element was upset by the Celtic, and what is the result? In the same way, Italy, where formerly the Germans were most prominent, is on the decline since they have disappeared. It is the same in Russia. There, if the national element outnumber the German, it will be impossible for them to maintain a proper state of affairs. Finally, your own country, Spain, owes all its grandeur to the Gothic blood. Our Hohenzollern would have infused you with a little German sap. The future belongs to the people of the North, and they have only commenced the glorious part which they are called upon to fill for the benefit of humanity.

HIDALGO : You will acknowledge, M. le Comte, that this is not very reassuring for the poor remnants of the Latin race.

BISMARCK : What do they think of us in the diplomatic world, M. Hidalgo?

HIDALGO : They think, and they say—as I now have the honour of doing—that you should have stopped after Sedan.

BISMARCK (*interrupting, and refilling the glasses*) : You are frank, M. Hidalgo. Your very good health !

HIDALGO : The same to you, M. le Comte; and allow me to add a wish for the union of all the European races !

AN OFFICER (*saluting*) : His Majesty the King, returning from his daily walk to the outposts, is coming this way; the Field-Marshal accompanies his Majesty.

BISMARCK (*rising*) : I beg you to excuse me, M. Hidalgo.     (*Exeunt Hidalgo and Busch.*)

## Scene IX.

*The* KING, BISMARCK, MOLTKE.

THE KING (*to* BISMARCK): Herr Graf, you will hear with pleasure the good news I have just received from the Grand Duke of Baden. Strasburg has capitulated. On the very eve, they organized at Baden an excursion train to go and witness the bombardment. His Highness has sent me some poetry that he composed on the spot. (*To* MOLTKE): Herr Field-Marshal, you will write at once to Krupp to make all the shells with the inscription : " *Gott mit uns !* "

MOLTKE : I will attend to it, sire; but if you wish this formula to produce its proper effect, you must allow us to send some of these shells to the Parisians. Never was this presumptuous people so squeezed in a circle of fire and steel, but they have a right to laugh at us so long as our cannons are dumb.

BISMARCK : I think, sire, the psychological moment has arrived. The effect of some shells,

added to that of hunger, must cause a disso-
lution, or a frightful panic, and in every way
will bring about the end of a resistance which
has cost us so dear.

MOLTKE : Only last night we had two thousand
men frozen in the trenches.

THE KING : Well, meine Herren, fire upon the
forts and upon all armed bodies, I am willing.
But, bombard Paris, destroy this home of
science and art, scatter fire and death among
a population comprising so many respectable
and inoffensive people! I tell you candidly—I
hesitate. I dread the moral effect produced
in Europe by such an attempt.

BISMARCK : But sire, if we stopped to think of
such trivial matters, there would be no more
wars possible.

MOLTKE : Allow me to remind his Majesty that
General Werder did not use humanitarian
arguments in causing Strasburg to surrender.

THE KING : I have this morning received letters
from Queen Augusta, and the Princess Royal,
which have given me food for reflection. The
Queen and Princess, both, are fearful of the
impression produced in England by this bombardment.

BISMARCK : If this be so, I urge your Majesty to
commence the bombardment at once. We
must to-day show the Englishmen how little
we care for their opinion; and to prove it to
them through the French, is an opportunity
not to be lost. And further, your Majesty
knows that Gambetta's troops were equipped
from English manufactories.

THE KING : They will find out later on whether
we have forgotten it or not.

BISMARCK : You fear to be accused of barbarism ?
Let the ideologists and the other fools talk.
Real power is only that founded on strength and
justifiable fears. Without hesitation, bombard
and besiege Paris; and every other place
that might be tempted to close its gates upon
us will think twice, knowing you did not
hesitate to throw your shells into the modern
Babylon.

THE KING : Are you very certain, meine Herren,
of the efficacy of a bombardment on a fanatical
population ? Our shells cannot reach over one
quarter the immense extent of Paris ; and I
fear their effect upon the besieged will be more
exasperating than discouraging. At heart, I
am doubtful of the opinion of Europe. Now

M

that the military power of France is crushed, and Russia has compromised herself with us, Germany can stand up against the whole world. But why assume a notoriety for useless cruelty? Wait a few days. Perhaps the Parisians, more inspired and enlightened by the defeat of their provincial forces, will surrender.

(*Exit the* KING *and* MOLTKE.)

## SCENE X.

### BISMARCK *and* BUSCH.

BISMARCK (*to* BUSCH): Sit down and write. Develope the idea that the bombardment of Paris has thus far been prevented by the influence brought to bear in high circles, but that such considerations should not prevail as against the interests of Germany. Show, on the other hand, that public opinion in Germany is aroused against the apparent inclination of certain states to intervene, and can only see in it an indirect encouragement to Gambetta. Reiterate, and keep reiterating, that public opinion in France wishes for peace—peace at any price and that the tyranny of the dictators of Tours and Paris alone prevents the manifestation of these sentiments. The English newspapers, through the *Times* as intermediary, must be made to understand that Germany's only desire is peace, and for the establishment of a lasting, eternal peace, she is obliged to take, on the frontier, a proper guarantee from France, whose turbulent spirit has been the cause of almost all the European wars.

BUSCH : Your orders shall be executed, Herr Graf. (*Exit* BUSCH.) ·

BISMARCK : How foolish are they who tamper with the liberty of the Press. It is so easy, with a little management, to make them say what we wish.

### FOURTH TABLEAU.

### SCENE XI.

*A German Battery.*

SCHWARTZ *and other* OFFICERS *and* GUNNERS, *then* RICHARD WAGNER.

AN ARTILLERYMAN : Lieutenant, we alone have sent already three hundred shells to those damned Parisians. Our guns are red-hot !

THE LIEUTENANT : Very well; stop for a while, say an hour.

AN OFFICER (*who has been for some time looking through his field-glass*) : It is curious; our shots seem to produce little or no effect. We start an occasional fire, which is at once extinguished. The greater part of our shells fall in the fields or gardens of the suburbs. Our enemy is made safe by its enormous proportions.

SCHWARTZ : Hallo! there is Mont Valérien saying good morning to us. Pif, paf! Two, four, six shells. Don't disturb yourselves; no one is ever hurt at such long range. Surely, if we waste much powder uselessly, our enemy can be accused of the same extravagance. This should be called *Much Ado about Nothing*, and might last a long time were not famine working noiselessly and surely, while we are amusing the gallery with the loud reports of our artillery.

THE LIEUTENANT : We, here, have the easy part; for you cannot improvise an army as you can an after-dinner speech. Since German heroism triumphed over the only real French army, that of Metz, the rest of our task has simply been a question of time.

ANOTHER OFFICER : What they have improvised, however, are their sharpshooters. The Count has ordered all those fellows to be shot.

SCHWARTZ : Let them shoot them ; I suppose that is the right of warfare. But I do not really see why we should treat them as criminals, when we thought our own sharpshooters of 1813 heroes.

THE LIEUTENANT : Schwartz, you talk like a socialist and a democrat.

SCHWARTZ : Ah ! lieutenant; I fancy that war is a field where democratic socialism grows faster than in the beer-gardens.

(*A huge* DEMON, *dressed in red and yellow, appears at the entrance of the battery.*)

AN OFFICER : What is this creature, dressed in red and yellow ?

ANOTHER OFFICER : A tropical grasshopper !

SCHWARTZ : A parrot metamorphosed into a man !

THE LIEUTENANT : Silence, meine Herren, it is one of the glories of Germany !

AN OFFICER : He is a curiously shaped beggar.

SCHWARTZ : And what a costume !

THE LIEUTENANT : It is the great maestro, Richard Wagner.

OMNES: Ah! Hurrah for the friend of the King of Bavaria! Hurrah for the author of *Tannhäuser!*

R. WAGNER: Hurrah for the noble and brave artillerymen, whom God has chosen to purify with fire and blood this modern Babylon! History, meine Herren, will relate in glowing terms the story of this siege, in which we have the honour to take part. What a glorious sight! What an immense theatre! It is the struggle between good and evil which is going on before our eyes, and in our own persons. Honest old Germany, too long ravaged, devastated, and oppressed by corrupt France, has risen in her righteous rage, and now, from the fortified enclosure improvised by the genius of our great Moltke, is inflicting upon the *Erbfeind,* with powder and ball, its well-merited punishment. The whole of humanity, seated around the world's great amphitheatre, contemplate with admiration this memorable struggle. The evil genii are there! Fire without mercy! Fire unremittingly! Saint Michael must conquer the devil, and the devil must writhe under his powerful foot, until he has surrendered his soul! Aim surely—here

—in this direction; there is the heart of the evil genius.

SCHWARTZ (*aside, to another* OFFICER): Oh! is he not cunning? He aims the gun at the Opera House, where they hissed his *Tannhäuser!*

THE LIEUTENANT: It is impossible, maestro, for our shells to reach the point you indicate.

WAGNER: What! Your shells cannot reach the unholy place where German art was scoffed at?

SCHWARTZ: Alas! no, maestro; unless you will order some other guns from Herr Krupp.

WAGNER: Well, the shells of genius will have to supplant Herr Krupp's. I shall put all this into music, and, after the victory, all Germany will come to Bayreuth to hear the last notes of the music of the future.

### FIFTH TABLEAU.

*Two Victims.*

### SCENE XII.

*The action takes place at Chelles, after the battle of December 2nd.*

*The* KING, BISMARCK, WOUNDED, *and* NURSES.

BISMARCK: We have fought two severe battles,

sire, but, thanks to the bravery and discipline of our army, we have gained two new victories.

THE KING: Two victories that have cost us much, Herr Graf! Ah! if those fellows were as well disciplined as they are brave, if they were less divided, and had better commanders, our task would not be so easy.

BISMARCK: Undoubtedly, sire.

THE KING (*to an* OFFICER): What are those curtains put there for?

THE OFFICER: To protect your Majesty, should the enemy see you.

THE KING: Take them away at once.

THE OFFICER: It was also to save your Majesty a sad sight. They are burying the dead.

THE KING: Take away the curtain. A King should not fear to look upon the effects of a war for which he is responsible.

(*The curtains are withdrawn. The* BROTHERS OF THE CHRISTIAN DOCTRINE *are seen tending the wounded and burying the French dead. The* GERMAN HOSPITAL CORPS *are doing the same for their fellow-soldiers. The* KING *removes his hat, and having for some moments contemplated the scene, retires much moved. The*

GERMAN AND FRENCH AMBULANCE CORPS *have disappeared. It is night. The moon shines coldly on the field of battle. On one side* TWO WOUNDED SOLDIERS *are waking from unconsciousness.*)

THE SAXON SOLDIER : Are they gone?

THE FRENCH SOLDIER : I see no one.

THE SAXON : Why did you not call out?

THE FRENCHMAN : I had no strength. Even now I seem to see everything as in a dream.

THE SAXON : And I too. Well, God's will be done. It is growing colder, and my wound is growing worse. Unconsciousness I hope will have the double advantage of hastening my death and diminishing the pain. Half my body is frozen, the other half is burning with fever. My God! how thirsty I am!

THE FRENCHMAN (*handing his flask*) : Here, take a drink.

THE SAXON : Thanks, comrade. So goes the world. Living, we kill each other. Dying, we clasp hands and become friends.

THE FRENCHMAN : Friend! Do not say the word! You would not accept it if I were to die a conqueror in Germany as you are dying in France! We are comrades in the grave; we are going to fraternize with the worms—that is all. That is why I do not reproach you for your share of the crimes of your sovereign, who has sown here ruin and death.

THE SAXON: Admit that if Napoleon had won, you would have done as much harm to Germany as we have done here.

THE FRENCHMAN: That only goes to prove what great fools we all are, and that our folly only equals the perversity of those who cause us to destroy each other like wild beasts.

THE SAXON: You are right, brave Frenchman. More than once since Sedan have I thought that our cause, having no more excuse of defence, had become unjust. But what we call national patriotism sustained and blinded me. Nothing less than the presence of death recalled my true feelings, to dissipate the mournful excitement of victory, to assure me that, conquering or conquered, Germany in this war will lose more than she gains. Under any circumstances there is an implacable hatred between the two countries. There is another war, with fresh crimes and more horrors, looming up in the future.

THE FRENCHMAN: As we on our side are not

altogether free from blame, so I can readily understand the fatal necessity which misled your mind and your arm. So I forgive you, and offer you my hand, although you are a Prussian.

THE SAXON: I was Professor in a University. Hardly five months ago I taught young men humanity and universal brotherhood, when I was suddenly forced to put into practice exactly the opposite of what I had preached. Before this I used to walk by the riverside every evening with my little girl, and my heart overflowed with joy at her innocent prattle. I gave no more thought to the French than if they did not exist, and I fancy this was much the same case in France. Notwithstanding, at one word from our sovereigns we have fallen upon each other, and destroyed each other like brutes. What will become of Anna, poor little orphan?

THE FRENCHMAN: What will become of my poor mother? Where will she get her daily bread? Who will protect and console her in her old age?

THE SAXON: Do you not see, comrade, that men are as idiotic, and fierce, and brutal as they were three thousand years ago? And the

teachers of philosophy—I am a case in point—
are not worth more than the commonest
labourer. Now, I see that when Napoleon and
William, moved by ambition or rivalry (of no
consequence to us), pitted us against each
other to fight like mad dogs, we should have
taken them and their ministers and generals
by the neck, and said, " Well, you are going
to fight, but without us." It is to be hoped
that the better advised future generations
will some day furnish a similarly grand example of justice and morality. (*Looks at his
companion, and sees he is dead.*) He is dead,
poor chap; he did not hear me. But what I
say is so true, and so many other victims are
saying the same thing now, that humanity, no
matter how deaf, must end in hearing. My
God! how weak I am! Poor little Anna!

(Dies.)

## SIXTH TABLEAU.

*The besieged. January* 1871.

### Scene XIII.

Baron de Montalban's *drawing-room.* Montalban *and* Louise.

Montalban : Will you believe it, my child ? these

infernal scoundrels keep bombarding the suburbs, although perfectly aware that they are only committing useless outrages, and not advancing by one second the capitulation? I have just seen a woman and child killed, at my very feet, by their projectiles. Ah! you will not surrender, hateful city: well, we will fire upon your women, and children, and old men! We will aim at the asylums, the schools, the hospitals! We will reduce your fine buildings to ashes! And the responsible author of these endless atrocities has always the name of God upon his lips, and in his blasphemous idiocy believes himself the instrument of Providence! And Europe coldly and impassibly contemplates this return of ancient barbarity!

LOUISE: Did you not tell me, father, that Europe was more powerless than indifferent?

MONTALBAN: Yes, but whether it be incapacity or a dulness of moral sense, it will, one day, pay dearly for its indolence of the present. I will leave that to the ambition and brutality of our conquerors.

LOUISE: Where is my brother now?

MONTALBAN: He started this morning for Chatillon, to attempt the demolition of a hostile battery. We shall soon hear from him.

LOUISE: God bless and keep him safe. What news from outside, father?

MONTALBAN: The last pigeon brought only bad news. The defeat of the army of the Loire is confirmed, and it is very certain that the northern division is in no condition to resume operations.

LOUISE: Then there is no hope?

MONTALBAN: There is still the army of the east, under Bourbaki; but I admit I do not expect a triumph, which the number, discipline, and strength of the enemy's artillery renders most improbable.

LOUISE: But in Paris there is a large force; why have they not attempted to break the blockade?

MONTALBAN: As you say, we have the numerical force, but scattered, without discipline, badly armed, and perhaps badly commanded. General Trochu is called upon to protect Paris against the Prussians, and the Government against the Parisians. He has the enemy stopped before our forts. I don't know whether he could do better, with such elements at his disposal. My patriotism accuses him, but my reason dares not condemn him.

LOUISE: Oh, father! it makes me shudder to think of this surrender which seems inevitable. I envy those who have died without believing in the possibility of such a catastrophe!

A SERVANT (*announces*): Captain Rollin!

LOUISE: I tremble for my brother.

## SCENE XIV.

### MONTALBAN, LOUISE, CAPTAIN ROLLIN.

MONTALBAN: Captain, you bring news of my son?

LOUISE: Where is my brother?

ROLLIN: Calm yourself, mademoiselle, he is only wounded!

MONTALBAN *and* LOUISE: Wounded! Where is he? Let us go to him!

ROLLIN: I could not tell you the worst at once. Captain de Montalban is no more. (LOUISE *bursts into tears,* MONTALBAN *bows his head.*) I also have wept. But let your grief be moderated by the thought that his death was glorious.

LOUISE: My poor brother!

ROLLIN: He did not suffer; he was killed instantly.

MONTALBAN : Where is my son's body, captain ?

ROLLIN : At the church of Montrouge, awaiting your commands for the burial.

MONTALBAN : Thanks, captain, I will follow you.

(*Exit* ROLLIN.)

## SCENE XV.

### MONTALBAN *and* LOUISE.

LOUISE : I wish to go with you, father.

MONTALBAN : Do not think of it, my child. It rains shells and bullets on that side. Stay here ; later on you can go, and carry some flowers to his grave.

LOUISE : But you are going, father ?

MONTALBAN : With me it is different. The bullets know me ; and, besides, I have no fear ; I am too much accustomed to their whistling. Stay here.

LOUISE : I beg you, father, let me once more see the face of my darling brother. After what our country has already suffered, is there room in my heart for fear ? I will keep so close to you, that if a shell should come upon us it would send us both to join him for whom we weep.

MONTALBAN : Well, my darling, wait for me.

(*Exit* MONTALBAN.)

A SERVANT : Mademoiselle, there is a man here who wishes to speak to you.

LOUISE : To me ?

THE SERVANT : Yes, mademoiselle.

LOUISE : Show him in.

### SCENE XVI.

LOUISE, *a* PRUSSIAN, *then* MONTALBAN.

THE PRUSSIAN : I have the honour of speaking to Mademoiselle Louise de Montalban ?

LOUISE : Yes.

THE PRUSSIAN : Mademoiselle, I am commissioned to give you this letter.     (*Hands letter.*)

LOUISE (*hesitating*) : From whom is this letter ?

THE PRUSSIAN : It—it was given to me by Colonel Petrus Walter.

LOUISE : Colonel Petrus Walter !   (LOUISE *rings ; enter* SERVANT.)   Ask my father to come here.

*Enter* MONTALBAN.

MONTALBAN : You sent for me, my child ?

LOUISE : Yes, father.  Here is a letter, brought by this person from Colonel Walter.

N

MONTALBAN : This person is very daring, and his master also. It is for you to answer, my daughter.

LOUISE (*burning the letter unopened*) : This is my answer.

MONTALBAN : And here is mine.          (*Rings.*)

LOUISE : What would you do ?

MONTALBAN : This man is a spy. He has not come here simply to deliver this letter. I am going to give him up to the Council of War, and they will deal with him.

LOUISE : Stop ! Did you not tell me that Colonel Walter commanded the battery at Chatillon, which is bombarding us from that side ?

MONTALBAN : Yes ; I have it from an ambulance surgeon, to whom this scoundrel dared speak of us. It is to him we owe your brother's death.

LOUISE : Well, father, we can take a more noble vengeance. (*To the* PRUSSIAN) : Come here ; fear nothing. We are more generous, even in our sorrow, than you in your triumphs. You will tell your commander that the brother of the lady who burnt the letter was this morning killed by the shells from Chatillon.

THE PRUSSIAN : I will repeat carefully what you say, mademoiselle.

Louise : Very well ; now, go.

## SEVENTH TABLEAU.

*The war, seen from above.*

### Scene XVII.

*The car of a balloon ; the Aeronaut, is watching the barometer, and holding the cord of the valve.*

Flitz, Didier, *a* French Captain, *the* Aeronaut.

Didier : Where are we ?

Aeronaut : I think we are about where we started from. There is no wind. We rise or descend as we throw out ballast or pull this cord, but we do not advance. The fog is lighted from below. I hear the guns. We are still over Paris.

(*He opens the valve ; the balloon falls.*)

Didier : We are over something. I hear a man singing. Listen !

The Voice : A friendly people ! a friendly people ! No more frontier !

Didier : That makes a pretty duet with the boom of the Prussian cannons. (*Taking the speaking-*

N 2

*trumpet and shouting*) : Shut up, you fool!
(*To his companions*) : And six months ago I
was just as big a fool as that!

FLITZ (*ironically*) : Evidently we are over Paris;
for only in Paris are they as innocent as
that.

AERONAUT : Throw out a sand-bag. I feel a little
wind, which will carry us eastward. Another!
The higher we go the stronger the current.

DURAND : I congratulate your machinists, Johnson; they have succeeded in this balloon scene
most admirably.

JOHNSON : Silence, friend Durand! While you
have been talking the balloon has been up, and
is now coming down. Listen!

AERONAUT : Are we down far enough, messieurs?
Can you make out where we are?

THE CAPTAIN : We have just passed the fields of
Burgundy, and I say with sorrow that I still
see some Prussian helmets. Apparently the
Garibaldian corps has not stopped our enemy's
march. I shudder for Bourbaki's army.

FLITZ : Are you still ignorant, monsieur, of the
real state of affairs?

THE CAPTAIN: Do you know anything new ? If so, tell us, for heaven's sake !

FLITZ : I should like to tell you less cruel truths ; but, while you were cherishing vain hopes in Paris, relying upon the provinces while the provinces relied upon you, the whole world knew full well that your defeat was an accomplished fact. All the French armies—or rather, all the bodies of men thought to be armies—are to-day beaten or rendered powerless. You know, perhaps, of the defeat of Chanzy, and the retreat of Faidherbe ; but you evidently do not know that Bourbaki's army, shut in by the Jura, can only save itself by taking refuge in Switzerland.

THE CAPTAIN : Paris will continue to resist, monsieur. If a miracle is needed to save France— well, we shall have a miracle.

FLITZ : Alas, captain ! the surrender of Paris was decided before your departure ; and even now you carry, without knowing it, the despatches announcing the fact to the Bordeaux Delegation.

THE CAPTAIN : Are you sure, monsieur ?

FLITZ : The American Legation was notified yesterday by the Government ; and the fact was so definite, so inevitable, that I was only asked to keep it secret until the departure of the balloon.

(*The* CAPTAIN *and* DIDIER *are stupefied.* *Some shots attract their attention.*)

AERONAUT : They are firing at us ! Look out ! gentlemen !

THE CAPTAIN : They are pointed helmets.

(*A couple of sand-bags are thrown out ; the balloon ascends.*)

AERONAUT : That is enough. We are now out of reach of their infernal bullets.

FLITZ (*who has been looking through his field-glasses*) : I think we can descend now. It seems to me that I can distinguish red trousers.

, (*The* AERONAUT *opens the valve ; the balloon descends.*)

DIDIER : Enough ! The wind carries us towards that plain, where I see some troops marching.

THE CAPTAIN : I fear you were too right in what you said, monsieur ; for these are evidently French troops, and their movements indicate rather a precipitate retreat than a strategic manœuvre.

DIDIER : They have seen us. Listen to their

shouts. Open the valve again. There, that will do. (*Shouts through the trumpet*) : Where are we ? What army is this ?

A VOICE FROM BELOW : Jura mountains ! Clinchant corps ! Army betrayed ! Bourbaki killed himself. We are taking refuge in Switzerland ! What news from Paris ?

FLITZ : Why hide the truth from them ? (*Taking the speaking trumpet*) : Paris surrendered yesterday ! Can we come down here ?

THE VOICE FROM BELOW : You had better go further ; the Prussians are too near.

(FLITZ *throws out some ballast. The balloon ascends*).

THE CAPTAIN : Did you hear, M. Didier ?

DIDIER : Alas !

THE CAPTAIN : Disaster upon disaster ! All our armies beaten ! Paris surrendered. Prussia gloating over the corpse of France ! Ah ! if despair ever enters a man's heart, it must be in the presence of such a catrastrophe. I will not survive my country.

(*Draws a pistol and tries to cock it.*)

DIDIER (*seizing his arm*) : Stop ! Faith in the ideas of progress and humanity has been the object and consolation of my life. Prussia has crushed it out of my soul. I will die with you, Captain.

FLITZ : You are two big fools!

AERONAUT : If you intend to shoot, be careful not to pierce the balloon.

DIDIER : Listen to me, Monsieur l'Américain. Before this war I loved not only France, but all the other nations of the world. I even wished Prussia joy! To-day I can only cherish hatred for the Prussians—a bitter, burning, implacable hatred, such as they have just shown to my compatriots. I acknowledge that this is an unholy, barbarous idea, unworthy of our age, our country, and our religion. It is the worst torture inflicted by these modern Vandals upon the better class of French people, and it is enough to make life odious and unbearable.

FLITZ : I fancy, monsieur, you are too reasonable, notwithstanding your just indignation, not to listen to the truth. Allow me to remind you that the same torture was inflicted upon the Germans by Louis XIV. and Napoleon I.

DIDIER : Granted; but that was half a century ago, and I thought that since then civilization had made enormous progress.

FLITZ : Alas! events prove that this progress was
more apparent than real. I am far from justi-
fying King William. To-day the Germans are
as blind as you were fifty years back. They
supplant you as rulers and conquerors. Supplant them as the wise, patient, far-seeing
nation.

THE CAPTAIN : Perhaps you are right; but such
sufferings as ours will not listen to reason.
Let me cure myself in my own way.

(*Raises the pistol.*)

FLITZ (*grasping and holding his arm*) : First listen
to me. When you are dead, will France be
better off? What! the French are unworthy
the great renown accorded by the world. You
are brave, noble, generous, capable of any
heroism—and any folly; but you lack the
strength of character which makes the greatest
power of a nation. You wish to kill yourself;
have you the right? How do you know but
that in ten or twenty years your country will
not need your intelligence and your good right
arm? France is now undergoing cruel reverses;
but it is the lot of every nation. Did not the
United States pass through an ordeal in the
War for Independence, when Washington,

without arms, without money, without a central power to sustain him, had a more difficult task to accomplish than your statesmen and generals? When your enemy has risen from the defeat of Jena, do you not insult France in saying it is crushed? No foreign power would think so, not even the Germans. And now her own children are in despair! Let me tell you a story. This took place after your disasters of 1815. France was beaten, as it is to-day, and had to pay a heavy indemnity. An old Indian chief,[1] renowned for his wisdom as much as for his love for France, received one day a visit from an old French comrade, who said :—" Great chief, France is in a sad plight; come to her aid, by showing us the rich gold-mines which you have never been willing to reveal." The old chief answered in a serious tone :—" I sympathize heartily with your country's sufferings, but if gold must save it, know that there are richer mines in France than in America. These mines are spread far and wide, and are easily attainable. Tell your countrymen to be wise, united, and hard-workers, to talk less and act more, and not

[1] Canadian.

only will they soon have paid their debt, but they will have acquired more real grandeur than they ever supposed possible." Does this interest you, gentlemen? Well, if, instead of caring to devote your time, your energies, and your intelligence, in promoting in France this old Indian chief's lesson, and proving what constitutes a true revenge, you still insist upon killing yourselves, I will not prevent you.

THE CAPTAIN : You are right, monsieur, and we thank you doubly, for having prevented a crime, and for having raised a ray of hope in our hearts.

DIDIER : Accept also my most sincere gratitude.

(DIDIER *and* CAPTAIN *seize* FLITZ'S *hand*.)

FLITZ : I will, gentlemen, prove mine to you in telling you some more plain truths. I have made rather a long stay in your country, and the French brain reminds me of a rapidly revolving sphere, in which centrifugal force brings all the qualities to the surface, leaving the inside empty. Let them be more moderate, and the void will be filled. Your countrymen are too often extremists, some believing in everything, others in nothing. Besides, they have no true religion; some denying God, others ridiculing him; fanatics generating atheists, and atheists producing chaos. Without religion there can be no respect for law. Read Washington's letters, and the history of our Republic. You will see what faith in God and a just cause did for our leaders in 1776. Let your countrymen read this history, and digest it. I would also suggest the *Bonhomme Richard*, and books of that sort, in place of the pernicious and declamatory newspapers which have heretofore been their ruin. And that is why true liberty has never yet found a resting-place in France; that is why America has such contempt for French politicians, even those who call themselves liberals and republicans.

DIDIER: You are severe, monsieur, but I admit we have deserved it.

FLITZ: Justice bids me add, that if you had become unbearable to Europe by your vanity, your conquerors by their arrogance are striving to become still more so. If they dishonour their victory (as there is danger they will) in re-establishing the rights of conquest in the nineteenth century, if they wish to follow in the footsteps of Napoleon I., they will learn sooner or later, as you just now have, the consequences of *Chauvinism*.

AERONAUT : Here we are in Switzerland !

FLITZ : I can distinguish the Federal flag. We can now descend in safety. Ah ! if France only would, how she could transform her defeat into a glorious victory ! How she could humble her enemies, without risking any renewal of hostilities, and without outraging any human or divine laws !

DIDIER : How ?

FLITZ : Simply by imitating this plucky little nation in its religious spirit and its true liberalism, and in giving a helping hand to lay the foundation of the United States of Europe.

(Curtain.)

# FIFTH ACT.

## Dramatis Personæ.

Johnson,
Jean Durand, } *in the Audience.*
A German,
The President of the United States, 1890.
His Wife.
Flitz.
The Emperor Frederick.
Prince Bismarck.
Trübe.
Baron de Montalban.
Louise, *his Daughter.*
General Walter.
Frau Walter, *his Mother.*
Wilhelmine, *Widow of Didier.*
Arnold.
The Delegates from the European Democracies.
The Diplomatic Corps at Berlin.
Schwartz.
A Socialist Workman.
Pluto, *King of Hades.*

CHARON, *the Boatman of the Styx.*

THE SPIRITS OF PLATO, SOCRATES, ATTILA, LOUIS
XIV., GOETHE, THIERS, &c. &c.

## FIRST TABLEAU.

### SCENE I.

THE PRESIDENT OF THE UNITED STATES, HIS WIFE,
*afterwards* FLITZ.

THE PRESIDENT: Our friend Flitz is home from
Europe; I expect him here this morning.
Have luncheon served in my study.

HIS WIFE: Will you let me take luncheon with
you, dear? I should listen to Flitz's reports
with pleasure. Of course, if you do not object.

PRESIDENT: Not in the least, my dear, I shall
only be too happy; you know that Flitz and I
have no state secrets. Our friend is an amateur
diplomat; he has undertaken the difficult task
of instilling some American common sense into
Europe. He will have hard work—even if
he ever succeeds. I willingly help him, and
can do so readily, owing to existing friendly
relations; but I, as well as the Government,
have no direct interest in the affair.

A SERVANT (*announcing*): Mr. Flitz.

*Enter* FLITZ, *who shakes hands with the* PRESIDENT *and his* WIFE.

THE PRESIDENT: I am enchanted to see you again, my dear friend. Well; what impressions do you bring with you this time, after your long stay in Europe?

FLITZ: Alas! my dear President, impressions which are not at all promising for the near future. It was not sufficient for Europe to have four great wars in less than twenty years —in Austria, France, Turkey, and the Baltic provinces. A fifth, more severe than all the others, is apparently brewing. What strikes me most forcibly in the actual state of affairs in Europe, is the cowardly apathy of the people, who (with but a few exceptions, which I shall . tell you of) support everything and anything with the inane indifference of a flock of sheep being led to the slaughter.

THE PRESIDENT: What I notice more particularly is the blatant folly of the German Chancellor, if, as you lead me to think, he is really going to tempt Providence by throwing his country into a new war. The world hoped for better things from the new Emperor!

FLITZ: The son of William wants peace, but

Bismarck and the situation are too much for him. When Germany imposed upon France the hard conditions of the Treaty of Frankfort, and took from Russia the Baltic provinces, she condemned herself to remain always under arms; and as a fatal consequence this military force must be made use of sooner or later. War is inevitable. Besides, Germany—or at least her statesmen—imagine they have not enough air, or rather water, so they are determined to possess Holland and Trieste, even at the risk of a struggle with Austria and England combined. Bismarck, whose policy seems to surpass everything in the way of human folly, still hopes to disarm Austria by compensations in the east.

THE PRESIDENT: If Austria allows herself to be humbugged again, she deserves—everything and anything; for truly, although the statesmen appear to see no divine justice in Europe to-day, it *is* there, and manifests itself plainly and implacably in every occurrence. Would Austria have been beaten at Sadowa and expelled from Germany, if she had not been an accomplice in the Prussian designs against Denmark? Evidently, no. Would the Franco-

o

German war have taken place, if Napoleon, in
1866, had not been Prussia's ally against
Austria? No. Russia, by being an accomplice of Prussia in 1870 against France, laid
the foundations of the war which so shortly
after deprived her of the Baltic provinces.
The fiercest quarrels are between the most
intimate friends. But while men fight blindly,
Providence directs the blows, which are sure
to reach the guilty.

FLITZ: Very true, my dear President; but these
ideas are worthy of a philosopher or—an
American. The Europeans would ridicule
them as pious, and characterize the person
uttering them as a Quaker, if not a fool.

THE PRESIDENT: But other reasons should open
the eyes of the Europeans. Can they not see
that the enormous expense resulting from such
extravagant armaments leads to complete ruin?

FLITZ: They ought to see it—and many do; but
if it is the majority, they have not yet the
energy to act. In the meantime, the national
debts of the European states are reaching
unheard-of proportions. This is not astonishing, for the money that we use in paying off
the public debt, and developing our commerce

and industry, with them goes to the support of a lot of soldiers, and the manufacture of new engines of war. Of course Germany leads in this dance of dollars. So, the new empire, which, notwithstanding the famous five billions, found itself poorer than France, is now, since the war with Russia, and from the necessity (more urgent than ever) of maintaining a formidable standing army, in a state of internal disturbance, the consequences of which no one can foresee.

THE PRESIDENT: I can readily understand the constant impoverishment of the German Empire on account of its military organization, and I know that almost the whole of the five billions was spent otherwise than productively, but I fail to understand the fatal effect the payment of this enormous indemnity seems to have produced upon the German people.

FLITZ: It is very simple. The five billions—or rather, the jingle of this colossal ransom—intoxicated the Germans more than five billion bottles of champagne. It provoked an increase in salaries and wages, and of course rendered production more expensive. Capital was used for speculation. Bonds and stocks

were bought at fictitious values. Then all
the great German speculators, believing France
irretrievably lost, and ready to disappear entirely when Bismarck should raise his finger,
sold French funds "*short*" in enormous
amounts; and to this imprudence, and to
French thrift and faith, they owe the loss of
the better part of their five billions. In this
way, political economy, sacrificed to the
science of war by the Berlin Government, has
gained for France its first legitimate revenge.
America foresaw this result; for, at the first
intimation of the success of the three billion
loan we recognized the vitality of France, and
our sympathies, up to that moment strong for
Germany, were decidedly changed in favour of
the French. These sentiments were increased,
when, at the Philadelphia Exhibition, we saw
the greater part of the space allotted to
German products and machinery occupied by
cannons and other engines of war.

PRESIDENT: You do not mention France; and
still, if I remember your letters rightly, you
made quite a long stay there.

FLITZ: France disappointed all the pessimist
prophets by her wonderful change of public

spirit and political enterprise. Verbose disputes made way for serious thought and a healthy condition of affairs. Vanquished on the Rhine, she has gained a double victory on her own soil and in the vast territories of northern Africa, now being opened to civilization. In this quiet way she turned aside the hatred of Bismarck, who, but for Russia, would have again declared war in 1875.

THE PRESIDNT : And John Bull?

FLITZ : Ah ! John Bull, so far, has been the cleverest of them all, for each time, without firing a shot, or even undoing his purse-strings, he has profited by the continental complications, in giving new outlets to his industries and commerce. All the same, John Bull thinks it will soon be his turn to enter the lists, and he is naturally very watchful of the ambitious longings of Bismarck for Holland.

THE PRESIDENT : But are there any definite indications that the German cabinet will be guilty of this folly ?

FLITZ : Yes, and here is a straw which shows the direction of the wind. Bismarck, some time since, brought into the Emperor's study a learned ethnologist, named Fürst, and said to

him : " Most worthy doctor, his Majesty wishes
your opinion on some grave questions of ethnological science, of which you are the shining
light. Tell us in few words what are the
limits assigned by God, through the voice of
science, to the empire of Germany." Fürst
answered, as if inspired, " Germany is everywhere where the German tongue is spoken,
where German hearts beat. Holland, Trieste,
a part of Switzerland, and Denmark, are a
legitimate part of Germany, as much as Alsace
and Lorraine, and the Baltic provinces." " It
is well, most worthy doctor," said Bismarck ;
" his Majesty thanks you, and will not forget
your advice."

THE PRESIDENT : The story is interesting, even
for us, for we have many Germans in America.
Fortunately the ocean protects us.

FLITZ : It is a serious business for the neighbours
of Germany ; for the same comedy is revived
before each grand war of the new empire. No
one can doubt the intentions of Prince Bismarck, who is the true ruler of Germany, since
one sees all the journals and newspapers in his
service accusing Austria and England of arming
with a view to disturb the peace of the world.

THE PRESIDENT: The old comedies always succeed the best.

FLITZ: This confounded Bismarck has upset all my plans. I had hoped to pass this year on my farm in Michigan, and now I shall probably have to return to Europe before long.

THE PRESIDENT: What do you hope to do ?

FLITZ: Ah! this is the other side of the medal, which I did not show you. This time I have learned that the German democracy has made serious progress. It has renounced political murders and the old communistic utopia; it has turned aside from its path of impiety and materialism, where so many European democrats have come to grief, and, strengthened by faith divine, it is bravely marching on to glorious liberal victories. Thanks to the follies of its rulers, thanks also to the wisdom of France, which did nothing to wound the susceptibilities of its conquerors, the common sense innate in the Germanic race has come to the surface. The democrat socialists are gaining ground at every election. They have made the Germans understand, that, as no outside danger threatened, it was time to look after internal reforms, heretofore sacrificed to the empty shadow of a blood-stained glory. And it is this condition of affairs which, crowding Prince Bismarck, will help to overthrow him, as an analogous situation did Napoleon in 1870.

THE PRESIDENT : That is a result which I hope for sincerely, in the interest of our European brothers; for, with France cured of her old conceit, and Germany wise and powerful, and rid of her military tyranny, which weighs so heavily, I think there would be but little room left for the follies of the other European powers.

HIS WIFE : How is it that the women of Europe do not strive to bring the men back to reason ?

THE PRESIDENT : Would you wish them to meddle in political affairs, my dear ?

HIS WIFE : No ; but each one could remind her husband, son, or brother, that what is unjust and inhuman between individuals is as much so between nations, and that God, who punishes thieves and murderers, cannot forget those who commit these crimes wholesale.

THE PRESIDENT : Very true ; and I fancy that many a European mother has expressed these same sentiments. But, alas ! truth goes slower than falsehood. Do you know the root of the evil

in Europe? whence come the lack of judgment, conceit, and the numberless prejudices
of which bad administrations and corrupt politics are but the last results? It is because the
fathers and mothers neglect to guide their
children's first steps, and most of those persons entrusted with this care will not understand that, before making a scholar and a
citizen, they must form a Christian and a man.

## Scene II.

### Johnson *and* Durand.

Johnson: While the stage is empty, let me ex-
plain to you what has been said about France.

Durand: Certainly; tell us how this miracle
occurred in France.

Johnson: I had prepared a grand scene, which
should come in here, and which would have
shown the beginning of the French regene-
ration. The Chief of State was in the midst of
an assembly called together for the purpose.
He dwelt upon the situation of the country, and
like a good President, eulogized each distinct
party, even those who were not worth a cent.
He called upon the patriotism of all, and, in sub-

stance, said,—" Gentlemen : Our dissensions
are the nucleus of our enemy's strength. The
more we reflect, the more we conclude that
these dissensions are caused by words, and not
by actions. The monarchists accept willingly
liberal institutions, so long as a republic is not
spoken of; even the ultra-radicals are not such
enemies of order as they seem, so long as the
words 'king' and 'monarchy' are not hinted at.
Each party has, like the bull, a certain colour
which infuriates and crazes it. In it, party
spirit and absurd prejudices play more prominent parts than principle or patriotism. I
have therefore thought, as a first step towards
a mutual understanding, that we definitely sup-
press the words ' republic ' and ' monarchy '—
a suppression which must be sanctioned, not
by legal measures, but by the patriotic common sense of each individual citizen. Let it
be understood, then, that we have among us
no more monarchists, no more republicans ;
but simply a lot of sensible Frenchmen, desirous of astonishing the world by their wisdom,
as they have heretofore scandalized it by their
foolish and puerile quarrels. Many words may
be suggested to replace the ones suppressed. I

would suggest a word which will do away with all party comments; a word suggested to us all when we see, across the Atlantic, that noble country which for the past century has furnished us such an example of good sense and true liberty. Let us call ourselves simply the French Union, and leaving out all wordy disputes, let us devote our energies to furnishing our native land with the encouragement it needs to recover from the effect of its disasters. Let us develope a religious sentiment, the absence of which has, perhaps, been a primary cause of our misfortunes ; and for the accomplishment of this, let us urge upon the clergy more indulgence, and upon the freethinkers more reserve; for their reciprocal exaggerations have caused the impiety and moral anarchy which have proved such a heavy burden. The example of America, Switzerland, and I may add England, proves — notwithstanding popular prejudices, some of which have lately almost compromised our success—that true liberty cannot be obtained in any form of government but with a religious people. In public education let us take a new departure, making it at once more religious and more practical. Having

taught a child to adore his Maker, teach him
to find in labour true enjoyment, and the
surest guarantee of independence. Work and
prayer; that is all I ask of the French people
in order to make their resurrection greater
than their fall. Guided by God, they will at
last realize true liberty—a liberty which gives
no heed to Atheists, and cannot be frightened
by Jesuits. They will no longer be the dupes
of meaningless words, and the prey of the
ambitious. I refrain, gentlemen, from en-
larging further upon this idea, which your
patriotism has already understood. I have
only opened to you a vista, at the end of which
lies the France of the future—a France more
glorious, more beautiful, than that, the downfall
of which astounded the whole world."

Durand: That is certainly a very pretty speech;
but how was it received?

Johnson: I tried to express the different sentiments provoked by this address. Of course
the extreme parties hissed and abused it, as
usual with fury, and it needed all the orator's
authority to quell the tumult. My actors
declared themselves unable to represent the
excited howling of a French rabble, and

suggested that I should give from the stage a
synopsis of this scene. That is why, ladies and
gentlemen, I have taken the liberty of address-
ing you. Let me add, that a French majority
having approved of their President's proposi-
tion, France, the country of Lafayette and
Rochambeau—our old sister rejuvenated—became known as the French Union, and began
to introduce into Europe the institutions and
ideas which have made the glory and prosperity
of America.

DURAND: This is all very well, and I cannot but applaud the future wisdom of my
countrymen; but your kind hypothesis is too
improbable. You have asked me to prompt
you; I will do so, in giving you my ideas on
the condition of France, from actual observation, and perhaps you will alter some of your
conjectures.

JOHNSON : Do so, I beg of you.

DURAND: Well, I believe that if the Republic
survives the gross faults of its partisans, it
will be through a truly liberal reaction against
those who wish, as it were, to keep the
Almighty out of human affairs, blind to the
fact of its stopping the source of all morality,

all power, all patriotism.    My poor countrymen
should think less of government etiquette, and
more of the government itself.    Some of these
days they will realize that they can no more
change national temperament than they can
the climate of a country.    If the sugar-cane
will not grow in the lake region, nor the
edelweiss be found in the tropics, neither can
an American republic flourish in volatile
France.    We might establish—and this would
be already something—a French republic
under the *tricolore*, but impregnated with
monarchy, bourgeoisie, and democracy—three
things as indispensable to the French, as
banners, flags, and flowers are to the religious
festivals of the south.    For this, the puritans
of the two extreme political poles would have
to give up their dreams, to resign themselves
to a mixed form of government, which the
force of circumstances seems to indicate, but
which can only be the result of reciprocal and
timely concessions.    Instead of your dream,
which is rather vague, here is mine: In 1890,
France will have at her head a President
elected and re-elected, whose name has rallied
all the tories around the new institutions,

while his well-known liberalism, his respect
for republican institutions, have made his
best allies, the whig majority. It would be a
republic wearing a cap of monarchy, instead of
the Phrygian bonnet, unless it were a monarchy
with republican institutions. In any case, I
should imagine a state of affairs in which
tradition and present necessities would agree,
as much as differences of education, origin,
and interest. would permit. This administration, as I understand it, would be actually
republican, as it would allow the French to
display their activity in any direction, with no
other limits than common sense and mutual
liberty. As dream against dream, Doctor, I
prefer mine ; but I fear we are both of us really
dreaming.

JOHNSON : Although we differ in our ideas of the
future administration of France, I see with
pleasure that we do not differ in regard to her
external policy and her liberalism. As for the
improbability of our dreams—all the more
reason why they should come true. Look
over the events of the past forty years : the
fall of Louis-Philippe, the return of the Bonapartes, the Crimean war, the unification of

Italy, our own civil war, the Prussian victories in Austria and France, the downfall of Napoleon III., the death of his son in Zululand ; was not each one of these events most improbable before it became an accomplished fact ? Patience, friend Durand, we have not an idea of the improbable truths the future has in store for us..

## SECOND TABLEAU.

### Scene III.

*A room in Montalban's house.*

#### Montalban *and* Louise.

Montalban : You have something to tell me, my child ?

Louise : Yes, father.

Montalban : Well ?

Louise : Yesterday I met Madame Didier. You remember poor Wilhelmine, who, although German, was so sincerely sympathetic in our country's sorrow. She told me that her brother, General Petrus Walter, was in Paris, and was most anxious to see me.

Montalban : Ah !

LOUISE : I did not see any reason for refusing his request.

MONTALBAN : I cannot imagine what he has to say to you.

LOUISE : Nor I. But I shall soon know, for I expect him every moment.

MONTALBAN : Then I will leave you. (*Exit.*)

## SCENE IV.

### LOUISE, PETRUS WALTER.

A SERVANT (*announcing*) : General Walter !

WALTER : First, allow me to thank you, Mademoiselle, for granting me this interview. Perhaps, influenced by your patriotic feelings, you have been a little unjust to me; but I, myself, love my country too dearly not to honour and respect these sentiments in others. Force of circumstances has separated us, but without changing my respect, my esteem, and—if you will allow me to say—my deep and sincere affection for you. You have suffered cruelly, no doubt; but do you imagine that I have not suffered—ay, and suffered deeply—when my only means of winning you was one which my

P

duty as a German, as a soldier, did not allow
of question ?

LOUISE : I think you are mistaken, General.
What could you imagine I hoped or desired
from you ?

WALTER : Would you have been so cruel to me
if, denouncing my sovereign's policy, I had
refused to fight against France ?

LOUISE : If you had done that, I should have lost
my respect for you, whereas, as it is, I have
only lost my affection; for after what has
passed, a marriage between a Prussian and a
Frenchwoman would be a crime.

WALTER : I hear you with sorrow, but with admiration, and I wonder how a mind so noble
as yours has not yet separated two sentiments
so entirely distinct as love and patriotism.  As
for me, I tell you frankly, you are still, and
always have been, the same to me, notwithstanding what has occurred—notwithstanding
your disdain and scornful repulse; and the
proof is that you see me here to-day, exposing
myself to fresh affronts in repeating to you the
sentiments so long cherished in my heart.

LOUISE : You are a man, monsieur, and a conqueror; nothing could stop you from con-

tinuing to love me. I am a woman, and my
country is vanquished—what am I saying?—
trodden under foot, abused, humiliated in every
possible way, and owing its existence to its
strong vitality and not to the generosity of its
enemy. Should Frenchwomen weave laurel
crowns for these men? Patriotism has also its
tender spots; do you not recognize them in
your country?

WALTER: You do wrong to upbraid me. My
presence here is all the more meritorious as
your rather ungenerous words were not wholly
unexpected. Should I have stopped so long
without seeing you did I not appreciate those
" tender spots " of which you speak? Twelve
years without seeing you—without daring to
remind you of my existence—almost without
hope; is not this, of itself, a right to your
justice, or at least to your indulgence? All
human mourning has happily an end. France
lives again. Europe honours and respects her.
Even we solicit her alliance. I dared to hope
that the painful proof, imposed on my heart,
might be over.

LOUISE: Go ask the people of Alsace-Lorraine if
they think the proof finished. Can you not

understand, that not twelve years but a whole
century of hatred has been placed between the
two countries by the dismembering of France?
How can you say that France lives again,
when a million and a half of her children are
direct sufferers from this action, and the re-
maining thirty-six millions only live in the
hope of delivering their oppressed brethren?
How is it you cannot see that the wrong
path upon which your government has started
leaves no security or guarantee to Europe,
and least of all to Germany? Ah! General,
let me tell you what has astonished me most
in all these painful events; that is when I
see in Germany, where beat so many honest
hearts, no one with courage enough to warn
your sovereign and his counsellors that they
have made a mistake, and that it is not in
imitating Napoleon I. that they will found
the true peace and glory of Germany. It is
glorious to serve one's country faithfully; but
when this country is in the apogee of its
power, when it runs no possible risk of defeat, one's first duty is, at any cost, to tell
the truth to the powers that be. I have
preserved my respect for you, Petrus, because

you have been a faithful and loyal servant to your King and your country; but how much greater would have been my respect for you, if, when our defeat was inevitable, you could have aspired to loftier and more humane sentiments, if you had used your influence to inspire your rulers with a just policy towards us; for a resentful policy, a revengeful policy, such as prevailed at Versailles and Frankfort, is not just, as it can only have disastrous effects. Ah! if in the midst of our sufferings they had told me this about you, I should have been proud of you! It could not have changed my duty, forced upon me by events; it could never have brought us nearer to each other, but I could at least have thought of you without remorse; I should have regretted you; I should have been proud of having been right in my choice; I should not have despaired of the future. You have lost, Petrus, your only chance of softening the pangs of our sorrow.

WALTER: Notwithstanding the harshness of your words, I pray God to bless you for the little crumb of comfort they contain, and for the ray of hope you have shed in my heart. My love and worship for you are greater than ever before. Let me, Louise, at your feet—

LOUISE: Stop, general! I see we do not understand each other, and there is nothing astonishing in this, as your most clever Prince Bismarck has not yet been able to discriminate between the good and bad, or frivolous qualities of French character. If you knew me better, there would be no hope mingled with your love. You must judge the firmness of my resolutions by my freedom of speech. I have loved you, Petrus, and I can now say I still love you; but you shall never be my husband. The fate of our two countries has for ever separated us. From the day when Prussia, by dismembering our territory, rendered reconciliation impossible, my resolution was taken. I resolved to prove to you personally, if occasion offered, that your men of state had misunderstood and abused our country; that we possessed a love and devotion to our fatherland, and higher sentiments than those of vulgar patriotism. I wish to avenge my country; I love you, but I crush this sentiment in my heart. Farewell, Petrus; I thank heaven for having allowed me to see you and speak to you for the last time. Perhaps my words may awaken in your heart a knowledge of those sublime virtues which Germany—judging by her actions—has never appreciated. You appear to be moved, so am I; but I feel that God inspires me, and I shall never regret the sacrifice I have made to-day, if it will but open your eyes to the light of truth. Farewell, for ever!  (*Exit.*)

WALTER (*after some moments' thought*): A noble woman! Ah! she has filled my soul with a new light. I had heretofore no thought but for fatherland! There are things beyond this; humanity, justice, truth! Ah! Louise, my eyes are opened. You will never see me again; but if in your retirement you ever hear of me, you will know that you were not altogether wrong, and that my heart was worthy of yours!

### THIRD TABLEAU.

*Hades.*

### SCENE V.

*The Elysian Fields in Hades. The spirits are*

*walking on the banks of the Styx. The number
of dead is so great that* CHARON *is continually
at work. At the back is seen a pillory, in
which* NAPOLEON I. *is confined.*

CHARON, PLATO, SOCRATES, ATTILA, LOUIS XIV.,
GOETHE, *and other spirits.*

CHARON (*landing a boatful of dead*) : I do not
know what is passing on earth, but this must
be the work of one of those wholesale murderers,
like the one in the pillory. (*Shouting*) : Take
courage, Napoleon ! your punishment cannot
last much longer ; for there is actually some
one on earth striving to replace you. Great
Jove ! what shall I do to bring this crowd
over ? Formerly my little boat sufficed ; now
I have an enormous boat, and it is so full at
every trip that we are in danger of foundering.
If this continues, I shall require from earth one
of those large steamers, of whose capacity I can
easily judge by the number of souls one ship-
wreck sends me. Unfortunately, it is easy to
come down here, but difficult to send a message
up there.

(*The boat touches. The dead disembark.*)

SOCRATES : Who are you, my friends ?

ONE OF THE PASSENGERS : We are Germans killed in attempting an invasion of England.

PLATO : Master, your sublime philosophical thoughts have not left you time to learn that the Germans are the Teutons and England the land of the Britons.

SOCRATES : Why did you attack England ?

THE PASSENGER : I know nothing, except that the English would not let us take Holland, and our Prince Bismarck, growing angry, sent an army to punish the English. The army was on two ships. Ours failed in its attempt to land, but the other must have succeeded.

SOCRATES : Who is this Prince Bismarck of whom you speak ? What nation does he rule ?

PLATO : Master, this Bismarck is a Scythian, and is Prime Minister of the Emperor of the Germans.

SOCRATES (to PLATO) : You told me that all Europe, without exception, was Christian and civilized.

PLATO : Alas, master ! it is true ; but the fierce passions of the human heart have been stronger than the divine light of Christianity, and the civilized people of to-day are, under certain

circumstances, no better than the barbarians of
our time.

(*Charon lands another load of dead.*)

ATTILA : Hallo, bloody warriors ! whence come
you ?  What giants have given you such horrid
wounds ?

ONE OF THE DEAD : We were killed by Prussian
shells, while defending the sacred soil of
Austria.

ATTILA : My name has been made the by-word of
wars and pitiless cruelties ; but never, in all my
career, did I destroy so many men as this conqueror now on earth.  In my time, armed
invasions of the south and west were a necessity.  To save themselves from starving,
our pastoral tribes went in search of more fer-
tile regions.  If such is not the case to-day, as
I hear ; if the soil of Germany is capable of
sustaining its inhabitants, why should they
leave it to spread desolation and death in other
lands ?

PLATO : Oh, King of the Huns ! the armed invasions of to-day—no matter upon what pretext
they may be made—are, in effect, more unjus-
tifiable than those of your time.  The soil of

Germany could easily nourish its children, but the ambitious ideas of its rulers will not allow the people to labour in peace, and quarrels with adjoining countries are inevitable.

(*Charon lands another boat-load of spirits.*)

A HOLLANDER : The fight is fiercer than ever. Amsterdam has suffered the fate of Frankfort. The Prussian General asked for twelve million florins, and threatened pillage unless paid in twenty-four hours. Some courageous patriots— of which I am proud to be one—opened the dikes, and the conquered city, like a ship that will not surrender, was swallowed up, with all its hateful conquerors, in the ocean.

AN ENGLISHMAN : A part of the German expedition, having escaped the vigilance of our squadron, landed upon British ground. The Battle of Dorking was realized. But the enemy's triumph will be of short duration. Not one of the invaders will ever see Germany again.

A GERMAN : One ray of light illumined the dark night into which our country is plunged. General Walter had the courage to seek the Emperor and tell him that he was mistaken,

that he was the dupe of evil counsellors, and
that the old affection of the German people for
his dynasty was rapidly changing to hatred.

A Voice : What did the Emperor answer ?

The German : The Emperor said nothing, and
wished Walter to go in peace ; but Bismarck
caused his arrest, and had him confined in the
fortress of Spandau, as Jacoby was in 1870.

*(A man who has been hung, the cord still
around his neck, disembarks.)*

A Voice : Hallo ! here is Herz, the leader of the
democrat socialists in Berlin.  How is it, my
friend, that you thus join your comrades slain
on the field of battle ?

Herz : While you, thinking to defend your
country, were dying to support tyranny; I,
with other faithful hearts, was working to rid
my country of those men who, abusing the
generosity and credulity of Germany, are realiz-
ing her ruin, I wrote and spoke aloud what
my conscience dictated.  I preached the overthrow of the Government, which is the scourge
of the land.  I was arrested, and condemned to
death for high treason.  But my death will
bear its fruits.  From the gallows I cried,

"The German people are ripe for liberty! Tyranny is only held by a thread, much easier to cut than this hangman's rope. Choose as your leader General Walter, and you will crush to the earth the dishonour and shame of Germany." The hangman swung me into eternity, but not soon enough to prevent my hearing the burst of applause, or knowing that my words had fallen like fruitful seed upon good ground.

SOCRATES (*to* PLATO): What is this group of venerable souls coming this way?

PLATO: These are the founders of American Independence. The most prominent in stature as well as renown is Washington; he who was the chief spirit in the defence and organization of the States. Around him are Henry, Hancock, Madison, Jefferson, Knox, and others; and last, but not least, the illustrious Franklin, who besides being a clever politician and a popular moralist, was a natural philosopher, and as such the first to teach mankind how to guard against the lightning darts of Jupiter.

FRANKLIN (*to* HERZ): Hail, generous spirit, the founders of American independence are proud to honour you as one of the argonauts of German liberty. You will, like Horatius Cocles, live in the grateful memory of humanity.

GOETHE (*to* PLATO) : Oh, most wise of all the Greeks, in the name of Germany and of modern society, I ask the pardon of ancient teachers for the sad spectacle now offered by Europe. I know that wisdom, the fortunate qualification of some men, cannot be that of all humanity, and that each nation in turn has been guilty of extravagant folly. But I own, I believed the repetition of such massacres an impossibility, and least of all did I imagine they would be the outcomings of a German triumph.

PLATO : There is no need to ask pardon, Goethe. The human heart is the same everywhere, and in its recesses may be found the serpent Python, alongside the spirit of charity. At this moment Python triumphs, but he is exhausted, and let us hope soon for the awakening of the divine energy of which this brave Herz has brought you the presage.

LOUIS XIV. (*to* PLATO) : Illustrious philosopher, I was guilty of many faults during my long reign, and I acknowledged the justice of my punishment in the pillory where Napoleon replaces me; but I assert that German fanaticism has accused me of more crimes than I ever committed. I broke my stick on the back of Louvois, for the much-talked-of devastation of the Palatinate, when many villages were burned, it is true, but after the inhabitants had escaped. In all my career nothing can be found to equal the sacking of Magdeburg, or some of the other atrocities now taking place.

*The back of the scene opens, disclosing* PLUTO *seated upon his throne, and surrounded by the judges of hell.* PLUTO, *calling* THIERS, *gives him a pair of pincers and a hammer.*

THIERS : What are these for ?

PLUTO : To undo the chains which still bind Napoleon I. to the pillory, and to substitute in his place the monster who is now ravaging the earth. Adolphe Thiers, you have rendered signal services to your country ; but a spite, unworthy of so grand a nature, blinded you, when, to crush Napoleon III., you insisted that he was the true cause of the Prussian war against France, and that Prussia was not in any way guilty. To expiate this, you shall yourself loosen the chains of Napoleon I., and you shall also confine in that pillory the Prince-Chancellor Bismarck !

## FOURTH TABLEAU.

### Scene VI.

*The scene is laid on Mont Terrible in the Bernese Jura—Four o'clock, a.m., July, 1891.*

Flitz *and the* Delegates of all the European Democracies.

A Guide (*accompanying* Flitz) : Here we are, monsieur, on the Mont Terrible. These piles of stones are the last remains of the camp established here by Cæsar after the defeat of Ariovistus. We are, therefore, on the spot you indicated. See what a superb panorama is before you ; on the left, the French Jura and the Doubs valley ; in front of us, the valley of the Rhine ; on the right, the mountains of Suabia and the Black Forest; Switzerland at our feet. We can throw a stone into three different countries. The sight well repays the tedious journey. Can I be of any service to you ?

FLITZ : Take the horses to that sheltered spot, and look after them.

(*Enter* ARNOLD *with a* GUIDE.)

FLITZ : Welcome, Arnold. Germany, represented in you, is first at the trysting-place. I thank you, and feel more sure of the success of our enterprise.

ARNOLD : The long journey I have made to answer your call must prove to you the confidence you have inspired in the Socialist-democrats of Germany—

FLITZ : —And which I shall try to merit still more; for, day by day, circumstances are aggravating, and the time has come when the Union League of the people must bear the fruits engendered by its long and untiring propaganda.

ARNOLD : I see on the different paths several men on horseback.

FLITZ : They are the delegates from other countries, whom I have called together, as I summoned you, in the name of the League. We are going to use all our thoughts and energies to find a means of restoring honour and peace to ancient Europe. I could think of no better

Q

spot for this supreme council. See over there the Grutli, which heard the oath of William Tell and his companions, and from which started the great wave of liberty which established Swiss independence. On your left is France, quiet, prosperous, having already regained her high rank, lost rather by her faults than her defeat. With the living examples of France and Switzerland before her, our deliberations may have more influence upon Germany, so honest but so morally degraded in spite of her military triumphs. While we are waiting for the others, look at and admire this sunrise. See that band of grey mist which covers the Vorarlberg Alps, and seems anxious to retard the appearance of the sun. In a few moments its bright rays will shine through, as the divine light of reason and common sense must sooner or later pierce the heavy clouds generated by passion and national prejudice. This band of mist has so mingled with the Alpine peaks, that it is difficult to distinguish one from the other. There are the first rays; see how they pierce the grey curtain of the horizon, proving it but an empty vapour. So shall the sun of justice and right dispel the clouds of Bismarck's hypocrisy, and show him to the world in his true light. Welcome, glorious sun! Thou hast shone upon many bellicose meetings! God grant that thy rays may light many such reunions of peace and concord as this of ours.

> *The different* DELEGATES *arrive;* FLITZ *takes each by the hand cordially. After some interchange of courtesies, the oldest* DELEGATE *as doyen calls the meeting to order.*)

THE DOYEN: Friends, as you have conferred upon me the chairmanship—so to speak—owing to my sad privilege of age, I must first inquire if all the Delegates of the League are here present?

FLITZ: I find Germany, England, Austria, Belgium, Denmark, Spain, Greece, Holland, Italy, Portugal, Russia, Sweden, and Switzerland represented; but I see no French Delegate.

THE SWISS DELEGATE: France has sent no representative for a reason which I am commissioned to tell you, and the justice of which, I am certain, you will appreciate. You know, gentlemen, the noble example France has set to the world since her defeat. She has devoted all her energies to domestic aggrandizement, and having surmounted many obstacles due to party intolerance or blindness, has at last shown to Europe the harmonious results of self-government. Having renounced the meretricious policy of the past, she now wields greater influence by her moderate administration. To the exuberant activity which sought an outlet in war she has shown a more noble and more useful direction in the struggle with nature. In this way she has opened the centre of Africa to the commerce of the world. France, unwilling to irritate the national feelings of the country most deeply interested in actual events, declined the invitation, but sends to the Congress her most ardent wishes and sincere sympathies, and is willing to agree to what may be said by the Delegates from Switzerland and the United States.

The Doyen : We first wish to hear from the brave man who represents at once the great American Republic and the Union League of the people.

Arnold : It is your turn, friend Flitz.

Flitz : Gentlemen, you all know the reason of this meeting. While Kings and Emperors are

exciting their people to fight we are striving
to accomplish a universal reconciliation. The
terrible events of the past few years—even those
now taking place—have changed the ideas of the
nations who have been the victims. In almost
every country of Europe to-day the Democrats
have wakened from their Utopian dreams to
prepare themselves by study and discipline for
a grand success. Almost everywhere, but
above all, in Germany, they have gained the
popular approbation, and can soon take the direction of affairs, which others have so abused.
Now they need only an assurance of their
strength. Well, the League has resolved to-
day to prove to the Democrats of Germany
their power, and to allow the Delegates of all
Democracies to protest against international
quarrels, and to assert, in an emphatic way,
their reciprocal sympathies in the bond of
interest existing between civilized men.

THE ENGLISH DELEGATE: As for me, I declare
openly, in the name of England, and of my
colleague of Austria, that the war we are
actually undergoing with Germany is only
defensive, and for the cause of general order.
We approved the formation of a German union,

but we became indignant when it grew aggressive, and threatened the noble little people of
Holland, whose neutrality is a safeguard not
only to us but to the whole of Europe.   We
took up arms to protect them and defend ourselves, as we did in the beginning of the
century to break the power of Napoleon.   It
is not against honest Germans like you, Arnold,
that we wage war.   In defending ourselves, we
aim at the destruction of Prussian militarism,
and we regret with sorrow the blows we have
to deal to so many of Germany's innocent
sons.

ARNOLD: Although a disagreeable truth, I admit
that our administration is opposed to justice
and the unanimous feelings of the people; and
I must add, to the praise of my countrymen,
that by a sort of patriotic abnegation, they
still put up with a system, the evil effects of
which they have felt more than any one else.
The war with France finished, the Socialist-Democrats, enlightened by the lamented Jacoby,
began to realize how dearly the German people
would pay for their triumph.   We did not
hesitate to point out the dangers of an administration which made of Germany a perpetual

war machine, able to support itself only by the blind luck of a Bonaparte, colossal annexations, or extravagant war indemnities. The wisdom of the French, which belied the prophets, obliged Bismarck to look elsewhere for what his western neighbour refused. He turned to the East and attacked Russia; to-day he is quarrelling with Austria and England. Germany is as sick of this policy as the rest of Europe. The execution of the brave Herz produced great emotion, and the day is not far off when we shall see the cup of German indignation overflowing.

FLITZ : Gentlemen, we are not common conspirators, and if this League has assembled us to conspire for peace and concord, it cannot intrude upon the exclusive right of each nation to govern its institutions and conduct according to its own ideas. The League has, however, thought it allowable to remind the Congress how easily the Federative system, as practised in the United States and Switzerland, does away with national rivalries, and settles peacefully all territorial questions. Take an example. How, without a fresh shedding of blood, arrange between France and Germany, the question of

Alsace-Lorraine ? Open your eyes and you will
see the solution of this problem in the immense
map at your feet. What means this beautiful
valley of the Rhine which God has stretched
from the Alps to the sea ? Is it for an eternal
field of battle for two powerful nations ? No,
when experience shall have matured European
reason, French and German will equally
acknowledge the necessity of making this
pasture-ground a neutral state, to serve as an
invincible barrier to all new aggressions. This
new State, the cradle of peace and liberty in
Europe, will be a connecting link between the
Netherlands and Switzerland, already eager to
join hands and commence the Confederation of
the United States of Europe. As yet it is only
a dream, but it depends upon you, gentlemen,
to hasten the time when it will become a grand
and glorious reality.

THE DOYEN: Alas, Flitz ! we fear that long and
terrible ordeals are between us and the realization of this lovely dream. None the less, however, do we hail with joy this sublime hope ;
and we wish to raise it so high that it may be
seen by all Europe as a beacon-light of safety
in future storms.

THE ITALIAN DELEGATE : Until the time that this federative tie consecrates the peace of the European States, let it be understood that the democracy must crush, in every land, all ideas of revenge ; that the use of force must be abolished, and that arbitration must decide all international differences.

FLITZ : On this basis—inaugurated by England and America at the Geneva Convention—I think that all Europe may clasp hands. The hope of liberty and peace will cause a universal thrill, when it is known how the delegates of the European democracies ratified the union of all nations, on the summit of Mont Terrible, hereafter to be called the Mountain of Peace.

THE DOYEN (*advancing and raising his hand*) : Let us swear to consecrate all our energies to the suppression of international prejudices, to the establishment of a lasting peace, and to the inauguration of peaceful and profitable rivalries !

OMNES : We swear !

## FIFTH TABLEAU.

### Scene VII.

*A public square in Berlin.*

Arnold *and others;* then Frau Walter *and*
Wilhelmine.

*The scene represents a holiday festival.  At the
back of the stage is a theatre, over which is
written, " The Awakening of Barbarossa."
An* Invalid, *covered with war medals, is fiercely
grinding from an organ the air of the
" Wacht am Rhein."  Other* Invalids *and*
Cripples *in the audience.  The curtain rises.*
Barbarossa *is discovered asleep, arrayed in
his robes of state.  His beard, which has grown
for several centuries, covers the ground like a
red and grey trailing moss.  The report of a
cannon is heard.  The* Emperor *wakes.  Some
red* Gnomes *issue from the rock and surround
him.*

Barbarossa : What is this noise ?   Has the great
crow-hunter come ?

A Gnome : What do you wish, master ?

Barbarossa : Go, see if the crows still fly over
the forest of firs.

*The* GNOMES *vanish, and, returning, begin a wild dance, waving dead crows over their heads. The cannon is again heard. The rock opens, and reveals, in a brilliant light, the* EMPEROR WILLIAM, *holding in his hand the broken sceptres of Austria, France, and Russia.* BARBAROSSA *embraces him, and gives him his sword and his crown, then lies down to sleep again. A few of the audience applaud. Others hiss. Dissensions ensue. A* WORKMAN *brings the crowd to order by his shouts.*

THE WORKMAN: These old stories are played out. We have been over-excited long enough by such historical reminiscences to make us forget our present evils and actual griefs. Let Barbarossa rest in peace, and let his successor be a better ruler! (*Loud applause.*)

FIRST SPECTATOR: Any news from Holland, mein Herr?

SECOND SPECTATOR: Yes; our troops occupy the principal cities; but, owing to the difficulty of communication, since the cutting of the dikes, they are constantly attacked by bands of natives, who are aided and sustained by the English fleet. Although there are no actual battles, we are suffering great losses.

FIRST SPECTATOR : Any news from Austria ?

SECOND SPECTATOR : We are also victorious there, but not with such successes as Sadowa and Sedan. We cannot hope for the much-wished-for peace, as the actions of the neutral powers are becoming suspicious.

FIRST SPECTATOR : God protect Germany !

ARNOLD : Did you ever notice, mein Herr, what happened when a large pike was put in a small pond ?

FIRST SPECTATOR : Yes ; he eats all the other fish.

ARNOLD : Well, the difference between fish and men is, that the latter, at a certain moment, unite against the pike and kill him. Do you not think this story put upon the stage would be more real than what we have just witnessed ?

THE WORKMAN (*to* ARNOLD) : Master, I think I am tired of these stupid plays. I have an idea for a new drama, and here is my fellow-worker.

(*He seizes a legless cripple, and lifting him from the ground brings him to* ARNOLD.)

ARNOLD : I know that face. It is my old work-

man Philip, who was so joyful at the prospect
of war with France.

PHILIP: Alas! master, I am well punished. A
French shell took off both my legs.

ARNOLD: And how do you gain your living now?

PHILIP: The Government pension is but a pit-
tance. I use my small talents in playing with
mountebanks and jugglers.

ARNOLD: An actor! without legs!

PHILIP: Yes, master. I can bark like a dog,
and am something of a ventriloquist.

(*The* WORKMAN *carries* PHILIP *to the edge of the
stage, and places him upon it with care.
PHILIP blackens his face with charcoal, and
commences to bark like a dog to attract the
spectators. The* WORKMAN *and some* SOCIALIST
COMRADES *knock at the stage entrance. The*
MANAGER *appears, still in the dress and
character of the* EMPEROR WILLIAM. *Some
of the* SOCIALISTS *drag him to a neighbouring
brewery, while the others enter the theatre. In
a moment the placard, " The Awakening of
BARBAROSSA " is replaced by " The Awakening
of* GERMANIA." PHILIP *barks furiously. The
crowd increases.*)

PHILIP (*in a guttural voice sounding from beneath the stage*) : Attention !

(*The* GNOMES *re-enter.* GERMANIA *appears wearing a golden crown, and wrapped in a huge cloak, which conceals all but a pair of shining eyes. As she walks a rattling noise is heard.* BARBAROSSA *wakes.*)

BARBAROSSA : What noise is this ? Do you bring me the keys of St. Peter ?

GERMANIA (*in a deep voice*) : No.

BARBAROSSA : Is it the jingle of the French billions ?

GERMANIA : No.

BARBAROSSA : Is it a new instrument of war ?

GERMANIA : No.

BARBAROSSA : Then what is it ?

GERMANIA : It is the rattle of my bones !

(*She opens her cloak, and reveals herself as a skeleton, the head lighted with a ghastly glimmer. With one bony hand she strikes the rock, from which a* FAIRY *appears.*)

GERMANIA : Good fairy, save me. Tell the son of the Emperor William that the happiness of the German people can never be realized if he listens to the evil counsellors about him. I want no more conquests, no more conquerors, but a liberal, honest, well-advised ruler.

(*Enthusiastic applause in the audience.*)

A SOCIALIST : The skeleton is right, but does not tell all. What has this cursed Administration done for us since we conquered the *Erbfeind*, and our other foes ? Have we grown better or happier ? Have we gained in the estimation of Europe ? No. The billions have spoiled us. The vices engendered by success have impoverished us. Our victories and our conceit have changed our former sympathies into hatred, jealousy, and distrust. We have been saturated with military glory ; but we want no more of this food used by the ambitious to nourish human nature. The German people aim higher ; first for liberty, which the vanquished enjoy, and of which the victors are deprived. We do not wish one man or one party to involve us in new and useless wars. We cannot approve in our Emperor what we despised in the French sovereign. We want an administration that will occupy itself in benefitting domestic affairs, that will increase labour, that will help the poor, diminish our sufferings, and raise the moral standard of the country ; and not a Government that sees only in the people a power to be ruled, or used as an instrument to settle its quarrels. We want no more of this exaggerated militarism, which leaves only scars and bruises—and those mostly to the poor—when France by a directly opposed policy enjoys the peace and prosperity which has left us. We do not want the world to associate this quarrelsome spirit—and those who are the brutal incarnation of it—with the true German sentiments. Germany only wants peace, to devote herself to science and art as formerly ; she also wants liberty and its human attributes. This is why we can no longer tolerate the execrable Government which oppresses and dishonours us. These are the sentiments of that part of the German union which our rulers despise because they fear it ; but which, all the same, forms an immense majority in the nation !

(*Loud applause and cheers.*)

SCHWARTZ : By the beard of Gambrinus, this fellow is right !

PHILIP (*shouting*) : Attention !

*The* SPECTATORS *turn toward the stage. A* PHANTOM

*emerges from the rock, with a cord round its neck.*

SEVERAL VOICES : It is Herz !

A VOICE : The first martyr of the German union !

THE PHANTOM (*by Philip's ventriloquism*) : Look, my friends, at those mountains of bleached bones ! They are the hecatombs of William ! There are enough to build a palace ! But thanks to Bismarck, with the hecatombs of Frederick, there will soon be sufficient to build a city.

ARNOLD: Hail, thou noble phantom! The memory of thy death will live for ever in human hearts ; it will mark the first awakening to our fatal system of government, which has scorned the rights of the German people. This Government, fearing to meet the just claims we might bring, has sent us off in every direction, in pursuit of ambitious chimeras and vainglory, which have covered Europe with blood. It has perverted the infant education, in inculcating a narrow-minded and exclusive patriotism. a spirit of conquest and hatred of neighbours. Bismarck has crowned this unjust and dangerous policy by crushing the progress made in popular feeling, and by re-establishing the right of

R

conquest, which for fifty years we have thought dead and buried.  The Administration has thus been wanting in the first qualifications of a civilized Government.  It has dishonoured and compromised Germany.  It has unchained the dogs of war.  If Germany—the Germany of Bismarck and his sycophants—approves of this policy, the triumph of brute force over intelligence and justice, free Germany, that of the democrats and socialists, protests, as it did through Jacoby in 1870, and as it does now in the martyrdom of this brave Herz.  The day will come when these protests will save Germany, and with the approval of the whole outside world ; an approval which she could not expect, if she were really identified with the unholy docrines of her actual governors.

SCHWARTZ : Another socialist right !  I should like to hear what Doctor Fürst would answer to this !

A SPECTATOR : They have given us German unity, but what is it ?  An array of bayonets forming from Constance to Kœnigsberg a hedge of iron, within which the German people are huddled like a frightened flock of sheep.  This unity may suit a Prussian officer, but not a liberal patriot. It was not for such a unity that we shed our blood. Is it unity, when we are starved by protective rights, oppressed by unjust laws, even deprived of the annual vote of the budget—an outrage which could not happen in any other civilized country? Unity without liberty is only a more effectual system of oppression.

(*Bravos and cheers, in which* SCHWARTZ *joins.*)

PHILIP: Attention!

(HANS WURST *appears with a pointed helmet surmounting the features of* BISMARCK. *He holds a large club. As the* KING OF DENMARK, FRANCIS JOSEPH, NAPOLEON III., *and the* EMPEROR OF RUSSIA *pass before him successively, he fells them all, and throwing himself upon their bodies beats them for some minutes.*)

PHILIP: Whose turn next?

(FRANCIS JOSEPH *rises, and the* KING OF ENGLAND *joins him.* HANS WURST *attacks them, but his club is now only a small rod. He looks about for another club, but finds none. The* THREE WHITE SPECTRES *appear, guarding the three sides of the stage.* HANS WURST *seems uneasy.*)

PHILIP: Are you afraid, Hans Wurst?

HANS WURST: No.

(*The* SPECTRES *approach slowly.* HANS WURST
*strikes at them, but his stick breaks.*)

FIRST SPECTATOR : What three spectres are these,
mein Herr?

SECOND SPECTATOR: Are they not the Three
Fates?

ARNOLD (*solemnly*): They are Justice, Good Sense,
and Humanity, who always conquer in the end.

(*The* THREE WHITE PHANTOMS *raise their right
hands. From every quarter suddenly appear
crowds of human beings, preceded by a cloud
of dust. The dust settling reveals the heads
--heads of dead people, the eyes ghastly, half-
opened, and expressing the anguish and
suffering of the last moment. These heads
are covered with Prussian helmets, French
képis, and military caps of Russia, Austria,
Denmark, and England. As the dust settles
the bodies are revealed as skeletons. The
skeletons join hands, each German between two
foreigners, and a wild dance is begun. The
noise of the bones clashing grows fearfully
loud, and as the interminable circles whirl*

*around the space in which* HANS WURST *stands grows smaller.)*

PHILIP (*ventriloquizing*) : Look out, Hans Wurst! This is not the hundred-thousandth part of those you have killed !

(*The infernal rout grows wilder and faster. The clashing of the bones increases to a groan, and then to a roaring tempest.* HANS WURST *is crowded, crushed, and finally engulfed with the ghastly crowd, which disappears in the earth, to the sound of thunder.)*

A POLICEMAN (*rushing towards the theatre*) : This is a seditious and anti-patriotic performance. In the name of the Emperor I command you to stop.

PHILIP (*making his voice sound as if from under the stage*) : In the name of the German people shut up, or you are a dead man.

(*The* POLICEMAN *retires in fear. Shouts of—* " Down with the tyrants!" " Hurrah for the German Union ! " *and cheers. Great excitement prevails.* FRAU WALTER *and* WILHELMINE *leading some of the younger children, all in deep mourning, come out from the crowd.)*

WILHELMINE: These are our holidays to-day! Ah! how different from formerly! O cursed policy, the scourge of mothers and wives, thou hast taken from me my husband and my happiness. Poor Didier hated Germany as cordially as he had once believed in her peaceful sentiments. I have suffered the pain of this cruel deception, which I believe helped to hasten his end.

FRAU WALTER: But for this, three of my boys would now be alive. There is no German family but what has paid this heavy tribute of tears and blood.

WILHELMINE: Have you news of Petrus, mother?

FRAU WALTER: Yes, he is suffering patiently in prison, where he was confined by order of the Prince-Chancellor. Notwithstanding the loyalty of his conduct, and his devotion to the Emperor, the Government cannot forgive his plucky frankness, and will only look upon him as the leader of the German Union.

WILHELMINE: I got a letter this morning from Paris. It is intended as much for him as for me, and, if possible, he must receive it. It will help light up his gloomy prison.

FRAU WALTER: From whom is it?

WILHELMINE: From Louise de Montalban. Listen.
(*Reads*) : " Dear Wilhelmine,—Before leaving
the world, I send you my last farewell. In an
hour I shall have made my solemn vows. From
this moment I shall have but one object in
life—to pray God to enlighten poor human
nature, and inspire it with better resolutions
than have obtained during the past few years.
I heard with pleasure that your brother had
come back to a more moderate and less exclusive patriotism, that he had courageously and
frankly addressed the Emperor, entreating him
not to enter upon any new wars, and urging
some reparation for the evil done to France.
I shall carry with me into my retreat a hope
that divine wisdom will continue to guide him,
and that the hatred which separates two generous nations will, by the efforts of such noble
and brave men as Petrus, soon be extinguished
for ever. To all your good family give my
kindest regards. It is not often that one of a
conquered nation can feel such lively interest
in another nation, who has so abused its
right of conquest. You can understand, and
do, how guilty your Government has been to
our fatherland. Better and happier days are

at hand. I pray to God that my small sacrifice may hasten the reconciliation. Farewell, my dearest friend—almost my sister! farewell for ever!—LOUISE DE MONTALBAN."

(FRAU WALTER *and* WILHELMINE *weep.*)

FRAU WALTER: Ah, my child! this is one of the many minute ways in which France realizes a noble revenge. In this manner is remorse created in the hearts of those Germans who have not lost all conscience. We may be superior to the French in arms, but they are superior to us in feeling and heart; and I fear that some day Germany will suffer cruelly for the false pride of her rulers.

*A popular demonstration is going on in front of the theatre. Shouts and bravos for the German Union and for* GENERAL WALTER.

WILHELMINE: It was for warning the Emperor of such results as this that poor Petrus was imprisoned. Such excitement among our peaceful citizens, I fear, promises no good. I have a presentiment that the Prince-Chancellor will not be allowed to be guilty of any new follies.

## SIXTH TABLEAU.

### Scene VIII.

*The* Emperor *and* Bismarck.

*The Palace in Berlin.*

THE EMPEROR : Here are serious complications, prince, which I did not expect. Just as Austria and England are almost vanquished, almost ready to accept any conditions of peace; just as we are setting foot on all the sea by taking Holland and Trieste, we are beset at home by all sorts of serious and unforeseen troubles. Is it true that the Liberals and democrats have agreed in electing General Walter as deputy to Berlin, to make a striking demonstration against the Government?

BISMARCK : I fear it is, sire.

THE EMPEROR : I hear that lately the democrat-socialists have displayed incredible activity in rousing popular opinion against us, and that their anti-national plots, added to the misery naturally resulting from every war, have misled our formerly patriotic people.

BISMARCK : That is true, sire.

THE EMPEROR : Is it also true that there is a tacit agreement between all the neutral powers, tending, by means of a systematic abstention, to paralyze and isolate us in our triumph?

BISMARCK : Yes, sire; but the situation, although serious, is not beyond our powers.

THE EMPEROR : What must be done?

BISMARCK : Exert in the interior, to begin with, a rigour which will awe even the most rebellious. The democrat-socialists threaten us. For a long time I have followed their movements attentively. The principal agent in this conspiracy is an American named Flitz, the same who, authorized by his German origin, and bearing a letter of introduction from an old American diplomat, dared, on the day after Sedan, advise me as to the conditions of peace. I have given orders for his arrest, and will have him sent to join General Walter, until they can both be shot—of course, with your Majesty's permission. We shall see, after that, if these socialists will dare to choose traitors for their candidates!

THE EMPEROR : Will that stop this universal coldness of the European diplomats, which is the most alarming fact for us?

BISMARCK : Yes, sire. The diplomats have doubtful, almost hostile, ways of dealing, because they believe us weak, because they think they see in Walter's election—which, moreover, is not yet an accomplished fact—the indications of a popular rising. When they find we are strong, they will respect us and fawn upon us, as they did after our great victories.

(*An* OFFICER *hands a despatch to* BISMARCK, *who, having read it, hands it to the* EMPEROR.)

THE EMPEROR (*reading*): Walter elected, and a riot in our capital! The people of Berlin would dethrone the son of William, the conqueror of France and Russia!

(*Another despatch is brought.*)

BISMARCK (*reading*) : "The rioters have forced the doors of the prison, and are carrying Walter in triumph through the streets."

THE EMPEROR : Have the strictest orders given at once, prince. Proclaim martial law, and make a terrible example of these conspirators.

BISMARCK : Rest assured, sire. I am not a parliamentary minister of Napoleon III. To-night, order will be completely restored. Let us talk of more serious things. The whole of

Europe threatens us. They must retreat in dismay at our power. We have already felt the effect of revolt after the war with France. The fierce strength of our attitude quelled the feelings they were disposed to manifest in favour of the vanquished. It will be the same thing now.

THE EMPEROR: And if they do not retreat, we can find in our patriotic energy, in our statesmen and generals, the material to destroy this coalition.

BISMARCK: Sire, you speak like a most noble prince.

## SCENE IX.

BISMARCK, *followed by* FLITZ, *then* TRÜBE.

BISMARCK (*to* TRÜBE): Take this yourself to the military commandant of Berlin, and see that the order is carried out in every particular.

AN OFFICER: Your Highness, a man who says he is an American wishes to speak to you on urgent business.

BISMARCK: Show him in.          (*Enter* FLITZ.)

FLITZ: Prince, I am the American, Flitz, whose arrest you have ordered. I wished to save

your agents the trouble, so here I am. Will
you allow me to ask the motive for this interest
you take in me ?

BISMARCK : I have ordered your arrest, mein Herr,
because you are conspiring against the established order of Germany, and because you are
in intimate and constant relations with the
enemies of the Emperor and the Government.

FLITZ : Your agents have misinformed you,
prince. I am, it is true, in intimate relations
with some Germans who do not approve of
your policy, but I do not conspire, and all I
have said to them I will repeat to you, if you
so desire.

BISMARCK : Well, let us hear a little of it.

FLITZ : Will you allow me to remind your Highness of our interview—the evening of the battle
of Sedan.

BISMARCK : I have not forgotten it. You had the
assurance to offer your advice—

FLITZ (*interrupting*) : Which you have not taken.
If I recall this incident, prince, it is because it
seems evident that Germany would not to-day
be in such a critical situation, if you *had*
listened to my counsel. You accuse the
democrat-socialists; it is only natural that

they should object to your policy, which is opposed to their principles. I have expressed my sympathy for them, but without joining their propaganda. I have said, and willingly repeat, that the power of the Government's adversaries would amount to nothing, if it did not respond to public sentiment and interest, if five dreadful wars in thirty years had not irritated, ruined, and decimated the German people.

BISMARCK: By your insolent language, you con firm the accusations against you. Officer! arrest this man!

(*As the* OFFICER *lays his hand upon* FLITZ, TRŪBE *arrives out of breath.*)

TRŪBE: Your Highness, your orders have been executed. Five of the rioters have been arrested and shot. The rest have taken flight.

BISMARCK: That was the only way to restore order.

TRÜBE: The rioting and disorder has stopped, but the quiet that prevails is hardly reassuring. From all parts of the city compact bodies of men are coming towards the palace.

BISMARCK: Do they shout or cry?

TRÜBE: Not at all.

BISMARCK : Have them fired upon.

TRÜBE : The crowd is unarmed, and the troops refuse to fire. The Emperor went to meet them, and was met with—

BISMARCK : Cheers ?

TRUBE : No, with a cold silence, more insulting and more significant than all the seditious cries. Here comes his Majesty, he will tell you.

## SCENE X.

### *The same. The* EMPEROR.

THE EMPEROR (*pale and excited, signs to the others to stand aside*) : Prince, the situation is more serious than I thought. I wished to judge for myself, and I fancy you know what has happened. I can always deal with an armed body, but what can be done against a crowd unarmed and silent ?

BISMARCK : That is simple enough. (*To an* OFFICER) : Tell the Chief of the Fire Department to turn all the hose upon the crowd. As they do not want fire, we will give them water.

THE OFFICER : Alas ! your Highness, the firemen are all with the rioters.

ANOTHER OFFICER (*arriving breathless*) : Sire, the rioters have invaded the Arsenals, and now occupy the greater part of the city. The troops refuse to move, and are morally in accord with the revolt. The palace is being surrounded. The telegraph wires are cut. It was with difficulty I brought you these despatches from the Minister of War.

THE EMPEROR (*reading one despatch*) : " The Army Corps landed in England has been forced to surrender unconditionally."

BISMARCK (*reading the other despatch*) : " The Austrians, in a severe battle, have routed the German army near Prague." Cursed luck! to turn against us just as we were about to crown the glory of Germany !

DURAND : This talk reminds one of the miller who killed his donkey by trying to make him live without eating, and who said, " What a pity! dead, just when he was getting accustomed to it ! "

BISMARCK (*haughtily*) : It is impossible for the Emperor of Germany and his Prince-Chancellor to succumb like a vulgar administration. I shall put myself at the head of the troops, and we will see if the mob dare advance.

AN OFFICER: Sire, the mob surrounding the palace have opened to make way for the Diplomatic Corps, who, having heard of the arrest of an American subject, have come in a body, led by the American Minister, to ask his release.

BISMARCK: Sire, allow me to answer them.

## SCENE XI.

(*The same, the* MEMBERS OF THE DIPLOMATIC CORPS, *the* DELEGATES OF THE PEOPLE, *and* ARNOLD. BISMARCK *remains standing, haughty and disdainful, waiting for the* AMBASSADOR *to speak.* ARNOLD, *at the head of the* DELEGATION OF THE PEOPLE, *steps forward.*)

ARNOLD (*pointing at the* EMPEROR *and* BISMARCK, *and speaking to the* AMBASSADORS): It is no longer the right of these men to speak or act for Germany. There is no more Emperor of Germany, no more Prince-Chancellor; only a couple of dethroned tyrants, who have a long account to settle with the German people. The dynasty of the Hohenzollern is over, here, as that of the Bonapartes is in France, under the blow of national indignation, and on the ruins

s

of a fatherland. The German Union will to-night be proclaimed in Berlin, and to-morrow through all Germany. Europe will not abuse her victory, as these men have so often done, but will agree to a serious peace, allowing all nations to join hands.

(*Hurrahs, bravos, and cheers for* " Peace " *and* " The German Union.*")

(*Curtain.*)

A GERMAN IN THE AUDIENCE : Your ending does you credit, Mr. Johnson; but allow me to say it is very improbable. Ah! you think things will go as easily as that in Germany? You do not know the Germans, and what is more, you do not understand human passions. William and Bismarck have created a powerful empire; they have united to crush Austria, France, and Russia, a number of elements, which, scattered over the different principalities, do not know their strength, but which, sooner or later, will use it against their teachers. United Germany is a dreadful child, who will eat his own father. Wait until the day of Germany's bad luck comes—as it surely will— and you will see if the Hohenzollern dynasty does not pay for the faults of William, dearer than Louis XVI. paid for those of his predecessors. Ah! I pity the poor Prince Imperial of Germany, and his heavy inheritance, especially as his praises are universal.

DURAND: I will not criticize your *dénouement*, Johnson, but will simply thank you for your good opinion of my unhappy country. I believe, as you do, that one of these days, common sense will come to the surface in France; but I fear the time is distant. Punchinello has a very hard life in Europe, and his death, which for you is no more than a scratch of your pen, will cost the people of Europe many severe and painful sacrifices.

JOHNSON: What you have just said is the secret of history, as well as the foundation of the religion which has civilized the world. I know not whether He who governs human destiny will see fit to carry out the ideas I have expressed in this drama, but I do know that I act as His faithful interpreter, when I show that humble and often unknown sacrifices, rather than the employment of brute force, have accomplished beneficial transformations in society. Thus will my audience better understand the epilogue of my play, which is this :—General Walter, elected President of the German Union, learns of the death of Louise, the day when the fall of the Hohenzollern dynasty assures to Europe an era of peace and happiness instead of quarrel and dispute.

(*The curtain rises upon* LOUISE, *the nun, rising to heaven, and blessing France and Germany, who are clasping hands over the valley of the Rhine, now a free territory.*)

THE END.

GILBERT AND RIVINGTON, PRINTERS, ST. JOHN'S SQUARE, LONDON.

www.ingramcontent.com/pod-product-compliance
Lightning Source LLC
Chambersburg PA
CBHW030640030726
47497CB00006B/1887